Andrew is the son of the late congressman.
Micki, a dancer for hire, would be the only reason
Andrew would survive the weekend.

ANDREW

THE CONGRESSMAN'S SON

RONALD DEAN DURBIN

ISBN: 978-1-63950-307-0 (sc)
ISBN: 978-1-63950-308-7 (e)

This publication contains the opinions and ideas of its author. It is intended to provide helpful and informative material on the subjects addressed in the publication. The author and publisher specifically disclaim all responsibility for any liability, loss, or risk, personal or otherwise, which is incurred as a consequence, directly or indirectly, of the use and application of any of the contents of this book.

Writers Apex

Gateway Towards Success

8063 MADISON AVE #1252
Indianapolis, IN 46227
+13176596889
www.writersapex.com

Dedicated to
Eileen Lenoix Bell Durbin

CHAPTER

On a dark and stormy night, Congressman Joseph Roggerro stopped in at the Blue Ribbon Gentleman's Club for a warm-up before heading on home. This gentleman's club was like most. Its name indicated the kind of clothing that was worn by the ladies working inside. One wonders if it would have been alluring at all if the lights were turned up.

Tonight, the congressman hadn't come here for the side attractions. He had one friend inside he needed to speak with. The seating was where you could find it. It was just past midnight, so the place was buzzing.

Joe was pleased with himself tonight. It looked like he finally had enough votes to get his "Organized Crime Bill" passed. Micki's familiar voice broke into his thoughts. "Congressman Roggerro, can I get you something? Anything?" The anything she said with a voice so satiny smooth and seductive that it would have started anyone's pulse racing—anyone except Joe's, well, at least for tonight.

With a smile, he ordered his usual. "Just a martini." As she walked away, Joe thought about a three-year-old who should still be among the living. Joe's wife and daughter died when they took his car over to Grandma's. They never made it. Someone had cut the brake lines.

Joe knew why they had died. He had refused to take a bribe and pass some pork-barrel legislation. Dale Jackson of Jackson and Associates Trucking had someone fool with his brake lines. The problem was that his wife had taken the car instead of him, and now she and Erin were gone.

Micki's perfume brought Joe back to the present. "Hey, Joe, are you okay?"

"Yes. I'm just remembering a little girl that would have been around your age."

"Are you gonna be all right?"

"Yes. Let me go to the men's room, and then I need to buy a dance." Joe just wanted to get away for a moment. Even after twenty-seven years, the loss of his two girls could still bring tears to his eyes.

Micki watched Joe walk away, knowing that there would be no dance. He would just try to talk her into some other line of work. Tonight, she decided, would be the night to start over. She sat his drink down and walked away. For a moment, she thought she caught some movement out of the corner of her eye.

Milo dropped the tablet into the drink and moved on out the door. When Jack was certain no one had seen Milo, he too walked out the door.

A moment later, Joe returned and motioned for her to come back over.

"Sure, Joe." It seemed as if she were almost purring. Her long black and silky hair draped down in front of her, covering more of her than her attire. "Are you ready for my dance? Or is there something else you want? Anything?" For Micki, *anything* meant anything.

She owed her life to this man. One night as he was driving up, Joe saw a man assaulting her. The man had demanded what she would not sell. Joe chased the man off and helped Micki inside. He actually had come to see her.

Joe had never accepted any of her offers, and she liked him all the more for it. She just needed some attention. Yes, she received plenty of catcalls and other comments, but that was not the attention she was after. "Micki, you are as attractive as ever, but I just need this drink and a few words, and I'm outta here."

He didn't see a stripper when he looked at Micki. He saw a young lady, one who reminded him of his own Erin. He fought back the tears again as he thought about Erin.

"Micki, aren't you about ready for a change?"

"I was hoping you hadn't given up on me."

"Here's a loan for $50,000 to get you started in some other business. See my friend Jere Durbin, and he'll take care of your legal matters, and I'll pay for them for now. I just want you out of this place. Deal?"

"Deal?" Micki's eyes flashed love, happiness, joy, peace, and then terror as Joe fell to the floor. He mouthed some words, but she couldn't hear them, and then he died.

From an office upstairs, a 911 call was made.

The only thing that Micki knew was that Joe was dead. She then took a deep breath and passed out. When she woke up, Nancy was talking to her and an EMT guy, Ron, was waving something under her nose that was burning. "Stop!"

He had accomplished arousing her, so he stopped waving the ammonia under her nose. "Are you okay, miss?"

"Where's Joe?"

"He's gone, miss. They've taken him over to Christ Hospital, but he's gone."

Detective Trudle interrupted, "Excuse me, miss, do you know what happened here tonight?

Unnoticed, a white Mustang pulled out of the Blue Ribbon parking lot. "Hey, Jack, do ya think the pill got 'em?"

"It worked its magic. That ambulance left without turning on its lights. I can already feel the weight of that fifty grand in my pocket!" Jack Veccillio was already making plans on how to spend all of his portion and a good bit of Milo's as well. Jack always helped Milo spend his money. Milo simply didn't know what to do with so much money, so Jack just helped him out a little.

The Mustang seemed to know where to go. It just drove over to Jackson Trucking, near Hoboken, as if on cruise control. The owner, Dale, had been dead now for six years. His wife Teresa had inherited the business, but it was run by Billy Ray Tolbert. The trucking firm was making money for Teresa, but Billy Ray was making a whole lot more using the trucking company to laundry his dirty money.

The guard, Tommy, opened the gate and let them drive in. "Hey you, boys, been out partying again?"

Jack knew better than to reply. He had just killed a congressman. Heads would roll as they tried to find out what really happened to him.

The room was dark and still, but Jack knew that Billy Ray would still be up. He seemed to always be up. "Hey, boss, you here?"

A light came on, and he answered. "Is it done?"

"Yeah."

"Don't say anything else. You never know who's listening. You two have done good. Now, get the hell out of town. I'll let you know when it's safe to come back."

"So where we going, Jack?"

Milo would go wherever Jack went. "We're going to Mexico for a nice long vacation. You going to give us something, boss?"

"I'll transfer it while you're in the air with some extra money to cover your expenses in Mexico."

"Adios."

CHAPTER

The on-call doc at Christ's Hospital happened to be Morris Becker, a longtime customer and friend. Nick was glad to see his friend, but why at 3:00 a.m.? "How ya doing, Doc?"

"Hi, Nick. Sorry to get you out so late, but we've got a problem. Step over here with me." Dr. Becker led Nick to a private room. There, someone was covered with a blanket. Nick knew the shape and size, and suddenly his heart was in his throat. "Listen, Nick," the words refused to come out of his mouth, and then they came, "I've been doing this stuff for a very long time, and I've never figured out how to do this very gracefully. I have some real bad news! Your brother was brought in about an hour ago. In layman's terms, it appears that he suffered a massive heart attack. He was dead by the time Ron and his EMT team arrived at the Blue Ribbon Club."

Dr. Becker was still talking, but Nick couldn't hear anything. His whole body went numb and cold. Nick forced himself to move over closer to the blanket. Under the blanket was his brother, his only brother. The world seemed to stop and Nick got off . Slowly, one foot moved in front of the other, and then he was there. His arm wasn't responding to what his brain was saying to do. Then he raised the blanket and saw his brother staring into nothingness. Nick just stood there holding the blanket.

Dr. Becker knew what was next. He had a chair ready for Nick to fall into. Now the silence was deafening. Morris really hated the next part. He would have to interrupt Nick's grieving to have him sign some paperwork. "How about some coffee? We've got some things to do."

Dr. Schloop broke in, "Dr. Becker, are you going to be a while?"

"Yes, Rachel. You're in charge now. Nick and I need to do some things."

"Okay, Doc. I can handle it."

Morris poured two cups of black stuff, and the two just sat there. Nick looked pale and hurt. His breathing was coming with great efforts. The two men didn't speak for a long time. They just sat there. After a time, Nick picked up a pen and looked at Morris. Morris just pointed to three places and Nick signed.

Morris knew that Nick couldn't drive right now, so he asked, "What do we do next, Nick?"

"I need to go home. I need to call Jere and have him meet me at Joe's place."

"Let's go. I'll drive you home, and we can call Jere on the way."

Nick was still numb, but he knew that the lead doc in the ER just couldn't get up and leave. "You can't leave, you're in charge."

With a proud smile, he replied, "That's why I can leave. Let's go." He hadn't done it very often, but Dr. Becker was leaving early. Rachel was finishing her second year of residency and could handle it. If not, there was always the cell phone.

So Dr. Becker helped the two-hundred-pound Italian-American to his feet, and they were off to Morris's jeep. Nick's home and bakery were just around the corner on Wright Street. He lived next door to the bakery that his father had started in the late '30s. Once there, Jere was called and agreed to meet Nick at Joe's place in about an hour.

Morris was not ready to leave Nick alone just yet. "What else do we need to do?"

"I need to tell Ellen."

"Sure, Nick."

Nick walked up the stairs and into the bedroom to f i nd Ellen, fully awake. They exchanged looks as couples do. "Why are you up and you know I wouldn't be able to sleep anymore," look.

"Tell me, Nick."

"It's Joe. He's gone, honey." He sat, almost falling, on the bed. They held each other and wept.

Nick knew that he had to start what he didn't want to start. He had to take care of Joe. He went to Andrew's room and woke up his oldest son. "I need you to get dressed. Joe has had a heart attack and has died. I would like you to go with me over to his house and meet with Jere."

"Dad, it's 3:30 in the morning. Do we need to take care of this right now?" Like many young people, Andy was thinking of Andy. He'd only been in bed a couple of hours. He knew the look on his father's face, and it meant *move*. "Can I shower?"

"Quickly."

Andrew didn't need a shower, he just needed help waking up. Moments later when he came down, three sets of eyes were watching him, seeming to know something but saying nothing. Quietly, three men walked to the jeep, for the ride over to 5 Dunbar Place.

When something terrible happens to a person, his body will do things to protect itself. In Nick's case, his body had given him a drug to relax him. Nick was trying to speak, but his mouth was not cooperating. Looking at Morris, he muttered, "Tell me . . . what we know."

"Ron Graham, our EMT team leader, said that Joe was gone by the time they arrived. The short version of the story is that it looks like he had a heart attack. We'll check that out. Ron overheard a policeman talking to one of the dancers. I guess Joe knew her and had gone there to talk her into leaving. She agreed to leave and Joe passed out. We'll find out why he passed out today or tomorrow. People are going to want to know for sure."

"Are you saying maybe it wasn't a heart attack?"

Dr. Becker looked Nick in the eye and asked, "How did he lose his wife?"

"Yeah, okay." Nick couldn't think about Marie and Erin right now. He would have to think about that later. It was very difficult to focus right now.

Andy was sleeping in the back seat and didn't hear the end of the discussion. Then the car rolled like a ship at sea as they entered Joe's driveway. Andy woke as they came to a stop in front of 5 Dunbar Place.

CHAPTER

Tim opened the car door for Nick with Andrew hopping out before Tim could get to his door. Nick looked back in at Morris with a tired smile. "Thanks, Doc. I guess we'll be talking some more?"

With a wave and a smile, Morris drove off, heading back to Christ Hospital and the congressman. The wheels of his mind had already begun spinning. He knew he wouldn't be working alone on this case. It was much too important, not to mention he wanted to know the truth for his friend.

Nick and Tim greeted each other as friends. Tim had been driving Joe around for the last eleven years. The whole household functioned more like a family than a staff. Saying that, Tim always addressed Nick as *sir*. "Sir, Mr. Durbin's in the study."

"Thanks, Tim. Is anyone else up?"

"Yes, sir. James and Beth are here, as well. We have coffee ready and Beth's preparing breakfast."

"Sounds good. Sorry you're up this early."

"Not at all, sir. There's nothing we wouldn't do for the congressman!" Nick believed Tim. He touched his arm and just nodded. "Thanks, we may call on some of that."

Andrew was wide awake. He wasn't quite sure why he needed to be at his uncle's house at five in the morning on a Saturday. For many young people, their universe revolves around them until that time comes when they realize that they are not its center. Andrew was nice, educated, and mannered; but he was still the center of his universe. So being up and about on a Saturday morning at five was not in his plans and thus not important.

5 Dunbar Place. Andrew wondered why would anyone live in a museum. He looked up and from side to side—definitely a museum.

Nick broke into Andrew's thoughts. "Let's go, Andy."

Andrew still balked at entering. He always wondered where all of his uncle's money had come from. Was it Mafia connected? Were bribes involved? How come elected officials always seemed to get rich? Why did his uncle always look at him in that funny way? Andrew always made sure he wasn't alone for very long with him. He seemed to like him too much.

"Andrew, come on!"

As if on cue, James opened the front door. "Good morning, sir. We are sorry about your loss." James Silver had tried to hide his feelings, but they were there. Congressman Roggerro had walked the walk, and no one knew this better than the staff that saw him with his shoes off. The staff loved their boss, but now their future was also on shaky ground. What would they be doing next week? They grieved over the loss of their boss as well as the probable loss of their jobs.

"Thank you, James. Joe will be missed by many.

"Good morning, Master Andrew." James Silverman had been working for the congressman for twenty-five years. But he knew about the accident that had happened two years before, and he knew about Andrew.

"Good morning, Mr. Silverman. Please. I'm just Andrew."

"Yes, sir."

James walked with them to the study as if they wouldn't be able to find it on their own. Andrew didn't like all the formality. He saw no need for it. Shaking his head, he followed.

Jere Durbin, Joe's closest friend and also his attorney, met them as they entered the study. This morning, Jere was very somber and serious looking. It took a good bit of effort for him to even speak, "Good morning, gentlemen."

"Come on, Jere! Is that how you greet family?" Nick was six feet, but Jere was taller and heavier. He grabbed his two-hundred-eighty-pound friend and hugged him.

Jere at first just stood there. Then, slowly, he returned the hug. As his arms reached around his long-time friend, his facade broke, and he wept over the loss of his friend and brother. This big, massive man shook from head to toe. Nick also cried.

The crying of two grown men was a bit unnerving for Andrew. Uncle Joe was a nice man, but Andrew still had lots of unanswered questions about his uncle.

Nick patted Jere on the back and said, "I need some coffee."

At that moment, Beth came in with some food for them. "Sir," she said, looking at Nick, "we have eggs, bacon, potatoes, muffins, and coffee. Is there anything else you'd like?" As she waited for a response, she began pouring coffee.

"No. This will do nicely. Thanks and thank you for coming in so early."

"Sir, I know he was your brother, but he treated all of the staff as family. Sir, we are missing him almost as much as . . ." Embarrassed that her feelings betrayed her, she left the room.

Beth had been able to hold her feelings inside until she began talking about her boss and friend. Many thoughts and feelings were racing through her mind. Her son had one more year of college, and Joe had paid the bills so far. She didn't know what she would do, including whether she would even have a job. In the kitchen, it was quiet. She was alone, and she didn't try to hold back the tears.

Andrew was in his own zone. He hadn't noticed Beth's quick exit. His attention was captured by the food. Suddenly, he was very hungry. He wasn't a big coffee drinker, but that looked good as well.

Jere was able to speak again. "I'm not doing very well this morning. I handle other people's problems a lot better than mine. I was supposed to be meeting with Joe today, and now here we are talking about his funeral." Silence again.

"Gentlemen, just enjoy your breakfast. We can talk in a minute." Andrew was glad for the silence. He also liked Beth's cooking, swallowing his food in the fewest possible bites. Soon his mind began drifting. He was awake, but barely. He wasn't quite certain he belonged here at this meeting, this planning for his uncle's funeral. His two brothers were home in bed with no idea of what had happened. Then his thoughts shifted back to his uncle. His uncle had always been nice to him. His Christmas gifts were always nice. It was too bad that he had to die so young. He must have been fifty-five. Andrew looked over at his father and his uncle Jere. Andrew was feeling just a tinge of guilt over not missing his uncle Joe like they were.

Julie interrupted his meandering, "Sir, are you finished?" Andrew handed his plate over to her. He thought he could get used to being waited on like this. Andrew closed his eyes, sitting there on the sofa.

The food had helped everyone calm down.

Jere was ready to move on, "Nick, we'll need to use Joe's house as the center of everything that's going to happen. I don't see this being a problem since Andrew now owns it."

With that, Andrew's eyes were wide open. "What?"

Jere looked at him and in a very calm voice said, "This house belongs to you, and this staff now works for you."

"What the hell are you talking? Dad, do you know what he's talking about?"

Nick was not ready to share everything at this moment, so he dodged it. "Joe and I hadn't talked about this. Jere would know everything. Let's listen."

Andrew knew his dad was not telling what he knew, and this pissed him off . Now, looking at Jere with eyes that were ready to attack, "Is it in his will?"

Jere continued to explain, "It's in his will, but it doesn't have to be. You're listed on the deed. You're on all of his accounts. Everything he had, he also listed you as part owner."

"And my brothers?"

"No. Just you."

Andrew was having a hard time accepting what he was hearing. His face was pale and at the same time a little red because of his anger. He was so angry that he couldn't see straight. What was it that everybody seemed to know but him?

Jere continued, "We will need to go to court to execute his will, but not right away. He gave his half of the bakery to your brothers plus two million to Nick. St. Peter's and Rutger's will be setting up the Roggerro Scholarship Funds. But everything else goes to you."

Andrew's anger exploded on his dad, "Am I the only one who's surprised by this? This is totally unacceptable! Dad! You knew about this, didn't you?"

Nick was trapped, but he still couldn't tell his son the truth. Not yet. Not at this moment. "Son, Joe didn't share with me any of his plans. He was a very private person. He would have told me if I had asked him, but I didn't ask."

While trying not to add too much more fuel to Andrew's anger, Jere felt he needed to continue. "Uh, Andrew. As well as I can figure it, you're worth about twelve million."

This final blow was more than Andrew could handle. " I don't want any of it. It's probably Mafia money or money from kickbacks!"

Now a very angry father slapped his son. "You will never talk about Joe with those kinds of words! That may be the exact reason why he is no longer with us. Do you understand me?"

His father had never slapped him before. Now he knew he had to get out of this house and never return. In voice and volume he had never used with his father, he replied, "There's only one thing that I understand, and that is that I'm out of here!"

CHAPTER

Stunned and confused, Andrew burst out the front door of 5 Dunbar Place. He ran down the sidewalk for two blocks, and as he began the third, he misjudged his step and tripped. For a brief moment, he was flying, parallel to the sidewalk. Then he made a one-knee landing. Rage had been replaced by tears, and now pain shot through his whole body. He lay there for a moment. His breath was coming in gasps. His whole body ached, with his knee throbbing the most.

Andrew wanted to get up, but he hurt too much. So he just rolled over on his back and sat up. His face was wet and now muddy. He looked at his hands and elbows, and they were scratched but okay. His jeans were torn and bloody. In the distance, he saw his dad coming toward him. Andrew made himself get up. As luck would have it, a taxi passed. With a wave, the cab stopped.

The driver looked at Andrew with a funny expression on his face, but only asked, "Where to?"

Andrew was relieved that he didn't have to explain his inability to keep his feet. "Please take me to 1826 Wright Avenue in Jersey City." There was no verbal answer, just a peddle to the metal. The rocking back shot pain through his whole body, but now he was on his way home. He hoped his mom would give him some answers.

Nick, winded, placed his hands on his thighs and breathed hard. He knew he was going to have to get more exercise. Andrew was gone, but Nick couldn't go after him right at this moment. He needed to get the ball rolling on the funeral and then go home and tell his son the whole story.

The cab dropped Andrew off in front of his home, well, at least his home for the last twenty-seven years. His parents lived next door to the family-owned bakery. He noticed that his brothers, Peter and Mike, had opened the bakery and may now know about their uncle.

As Andrew entered the house, he began calling his mom. The house seemed empty, so he headed up the stairs. There he found his mother in the attic. She too was crying, with her face in her hands. Tissues lay all around.

"Mom, are you okay?" His rage left as he moved off center and focused on his mother.

Her response startled him. It was clear and quick! "No, son, I'm not. First, my friend Marie and her daughter Erin die at the hands of some very mean people, and now maybe these same people have taken Joe." As she spoke, the tears began to flow and her voice began to quiver, but she continued on. "No. Andrew, I'm not okay. People can't get away with stuff like this!"

"Here. Take a look at this." She handed the 8 x 10 to him.

Andrew's mother's sadness took him out of his own pity party and made him think about her needs. "Who are these people? Is that Uncle Joe?"

"That's Uncle Joe, his wife, Marie, and their daughter, Erin." Andrew wasn't in the photo because he hadn't arrived yet. For a few moments, he just looked, studying this family.

Then he caught his reflection in the mirror. He studied some more. Ellen sat quietly as the revelation occurred. Then she handed a small photo of the same family but with a newborn.

Mother and son looked at each other, and she spoke first. "Yes, honey, that's you."

Nick was only able get the process started, and then he had to leave. He arrived in the attic just as Ellen was telling her son.

Andrew checked his image in the mirror and then looked back at the photo.

Then Nick spoke, "You look a lot like your father, but you have your mother's eyes."

Andrew wasn't sure what he was feeling, but involuntarily, rage swelled up inside him over his father's deception. "Why didn't you tell me this at Joe's house? Instead, you lied to me!"

If eyes could hurt you, then Nick would have been in trouble. "At the time you didn't seem like you were ready to listen."

"Bullshit! How about some truth?"

Ellen acted offended. "Andrew." Then looking at her husband. "Are you ready to tell our son some truth?"

Nick was ready. He had carried the secret for twenty-seven years, and now it would no longer be a secret. "Joe was elected to Congress about twenty-seven years ago. Some thugs offered him a bribe to pass some pork-barrel legislation. He told them where to go and to take lots of ice. Three days later, his wife and daughter were dead because of bad brakes. They weren't cut, just loosened. When Marie and Erin drove over to Grandma's, they never returned, alive. The short version of the story is that Joe felt it was his mission in life to be a congressman, but he was not going to risk your life. He asked us to adopt you and keep you safe. He watched you grow up from a distance."

He knew his son heard the story, but it was unacceptable to him. Andrew's eyes were boring into Nick. "I don't know if you will hear this now or not. But the fact that Joe was your father doesn't mean that you are any less my son. You were and still are my son."

Andrew was on overload. He couldn't deal with one more thing. Nick started toward him, but Andrew held up his hand to stop Nick's movement. Dazed, Andrew left the attic and headed for his room. His mind seemed to be on cruise control as he undressed. His knee and his pants didn't like parting company. The clothes just fell to the floor. The hot water felt great. It stung the knee, but Andrew needed the shower, the time to think. His head ached along with his knee. The shower ran and ran. Finally, he made himself turn it off . Then slowly he moved out of the shower and back into his new world. He was very weak now, so he just sat on the bed.

Andrew wasn't sure what time it was when he opened his eyes, but he felt better. Then he tried to move. His body was a little stiff, but his knee ached. The last time he got out of bed, his life changed dramatically. He just wanted to go back to bed and forget about all that had happened. This morning at four, life was good and simple. How things can change. He thought he would need a big patch for his knee, and then he would just leave the house for a while.

It was just past one as Andrew was walking out of the house. He decided to get a cup of coffee at the bakery. His brothers looked at him a little weird, so he knew they knew. "Dad tell you?"

Peter answered, "No, Mom."

"I'm going to get some coffee and hit the road for a while."

Mike wanted to help in some way but didn't know exactly how to, so he replied, "No problem. We've got things covered." To Mike, it sounded corny and canned. He looked down and just shook his head.

"See ya." With that, Andrew was off down the walk. Then he turned around and decided to drive his silver Bug instead of walking. He now knew where he was going.

Billy Ray Tolbert believed Jack when he told him that the congressman had been taken care of. What bothered Toll was whether there were any loose ends. Jack and Milo were heading to Mexico for a few weeks just to make sure that they didn't slip up and reveal anything.

Toll thought to himself that it might be time for Jack and Milo to turn up missing. Toll remembered fixing the brakes on the congressman's car some twenty-seven years ago. More recently, he had adjusted his boss's brakes and had to console a grieving Mrs. Jackson. She made a big mistake by trusting Toll to run her husband's trucking company. Toll had taken the company deeper and deeper into organized crime. Toll let out an evil laugh as he thought about how stupid the world was. How stupid Teresa Jackson was for giving him free rein within the company.

The congressman was stupid for not accepting Dale's financial offer. No! The congressman had to act like some Boy Scout. Toll thought about the two ladies that died instead of Roggerro, but that was okay. It was just part of the business. Killing Dale Jackson was just part of Toll's business. Toll, speaking to no one, said, "Now I'm the boss. That fool told me not to trust anyone, and he trusted me. Oh well, we all gotta go some time." His laughter grew as he thought about the irony of the whole thing.

Actually, it was Toll's insanity that was growing. The sleepless nights and his abuse of alcohol and other drugs were having their affect. Even Sharon, his long-time girlfriend, couldn't satisfy or comfort him any longer. Pug kept finding "ladies" that were willing to do most anything with someone who looked and acted rich. He still hadn't found the right girl to replace Sharon, just yet.

It was Pug's name that Toll screamed for. "Hey, Pug! I'll need you to stay by the phone tonight. I'm going out, and I may need Danny and Vinnie to do a little job for me."

Pug always agreed and smiled when his boss spoke. "Yeah. Sure thing, Toll. I got nothin' else goin'. You want I should have something waitin' for you when you get back?"

His insane anger flared and then clicked off . "Not tonight." He slipped on his jacket and headed for the door. He always tried to dress above his station in life which in turn always made him look foolish. For many of the same reasons, he liked driving big cars. The ads had said, "Feel like a king. Drive like a king. Just be the king." In his insanity, it all made sense.

He was happy and miserable at the same time. His power made him happy. He loved stepping on people, and so for a little while, he would be happy that he had taken out the congressman. That crime bill would have been able to track his money, virtually shutting down his operation. For now, there was no Roggerro and no crime bill.

He sat down in Blue and indeed felt like a king. He opened the garage door and drove out his private entrance, befitting someone of his position. He called his Caddy, Blue. Toll headed for the turnpike and the Blue Ribbon Club.

George Williams owned and operated the Blue Ribbon. It was his only source of income, so he watched it closely. Williams seldom took a night off . He might not be on the floor, but he would be watching. He was watching the night before, when those two dropped something into the congressman's drink. Within minutes of him drinking it, he fell to the floor. George had been the one to call 911. The police had already been by and seemed to be satisfied. There would be nothing to gain by revealing to the police what he saw. And there might be a lot to lose, like his life. If someone was bold enough to go after a United States congressman, then they would think nothing at all about killing the owner of a gentleman's club.

Gentleman's club sounded much nicer than *Williams Strip Joint*, which in fact it was. But by calling it a gentleman's club, he could advertise on the radio and in papers without so much as a batted eye.

Williams was watching as Toll entered and took a table in the far corner. That was almost the same place where those other two had sat the previous night. I might need to keep an eye on this guy, he thought.

Toll, on the other hand, had thought that he had gotten in unnoticed. *Sitting back in this dark corner, not even the waitress can make me,* and he smiled. *What was the girl's name who had waited on the congressman? Micki. I'll keep an eye on her and see if she acts strange or talks to anyone for too long.*

Several girls came by and offered to stay for a price, but none used Micki as her name. Finally, Toll had one stay, and they talked about the night before. "How terrible! A U.S. congressman dying right here. How'd it happen?"

"Mister, if you want to use your time talking, that's fine with me, but I'm on the clock."

"I'm just so, what, amazed. He died right here. Did you see it?"

"No, Micki was with him. She saw him fall. Then she passed out too."

"Could I talk with this Micki?"

"Oh she won't be coming in till later, much later."

With the bit of information, Toll knew that this conversation was over. He paid her the forty, and she was off. This was all a lot of trouble.

None of this would have been necessary if that damn congressman had left well enough alone. *His damn bill was going to make it possible for the feds to track my money.* Toll's insanity consumed a little more of reality each hour. Never mind that he and his organized crime friends were killing people and ruining lives by various means, it was the congressman who was at fault. A few of Toll's rats had already jumped ship and others were preparing to. All Toll could see was today, and today was better because a congressman had died. An evil laugh almost escaped his mouth. He actually slapped himself covering his mouth. Now talking to himself, *Wait, you fool, until we are out in the car.*

His mind was playing over and over again. *No damn bill and no damn congressman.* Toll knew he would have to leave. The Toll that wanted to shout and laugh was winning over the Toll that wanted to wait and watch.

No one noticed Toll's departure except George.

The investigating officer for Congressman Roggerro's case was Detective Johnny Trudle. He had asked for it as soon as he got word of what had gone down. Johnny's older sister, Marie, had married Joe; and it seemed like they were a perfect match. First, Erin came along and then little Andy. Life was perfect until the "accident." The police couldn't find any proof that tied anyone to it. On that day, Johnny vowed to become a policeman and find that elusive proof that would lock up criminals. Johnny had been finding those connections for the last twenty-five years. Sometimes his methods had gotten him into trouble, but he had landed on his feet thus far.

Chief Molar called a meeting with Johnny. "I'm probably making a mistake by letting you take this case. You're too close to it. You're sometimes too relentless. You do too much damage getting to the bad guys. Damn it, Trudle, you're a great cop who just doesn't know when to stop. On this case, the nation will be watching and if there is the slightest hint that you are about to get out of bounds, you'll be off this case and the force. Am I clear?"

Not waiting for an answer but now looking at Sergeant Douglas, he said, "Sergeant, don't let him get you in trouble or I'll have your badge as well!"

Christi had heard this line before. Johnny was a little rough, but he always got results. She also knew that this case would be different. It had become personal with Johnny. For a cop, that's bad. Lines of right and wrong become blurred and fuzzy, and it's too easy to cross the line to take care of something personal.

Call it a hunch, instinct, ESP, or whatever. Johnny knew that Joe hadn't died from a heart attack. Now he just needed to find out what had happened. On his first visit to the club, he acted very content with all that was happening. He wanted the bad guys to relax and make their mistakes. The truth would come out. He just needed to be patient. People knew things that they weren't talking about just yet, but they would.

The autopsy hadn't revealed anything. They wanted to write that the cause of death was a heart attack, but Johnny convinced them not to list the cause of death. The report read that the cause of death was still under investigation. Joe had been healthy. He was 5'11" and 220 pounds. Everything was normal for a man of his size and age. Johnny had remained best friends with Joe. He told himself he would find the connection.

CHAPTER

As Andrew entered the New Jersey turnpike, he heard the first public statement about his father's death. "We interrupt this program to bring you a news bulletin. The Jersey City Coroner's Office has just confirmed that Congressman Joseph J. Roggerro is dead at the age of fifty-eight. It appears that the congressman succumbed to a fatal heart attack while having a drink at a local club. Once again, let me repeat. Congressman Joseph Roggerro was dead on arrival at Christ's Hospital at 1:30 a.m. this morning. We'll be following this story all afternoon, so stay tuned . . ."

Andrew's thoughts began wondering if his father was right about his father. That one thought made him shake his head. The VW turned off the turnpike and headed downtown. Andrew had his hands on the wheel, but the silver Bug seemed to know where to go, and then he parked.

As he walked in the big double doors of the Jersey City Police Station, he could still hear his mother's voice. "No, Andrew. I'm not okay! It's not fair. People can't get away with stuff like this."

Andrew was looking around like a kid in a toy store when Sergeant Trujillo asked, "How can I help you, young man?"

"Uh, well. Do you have someone assigned to the congressman's death?"

"Yes, we do. That would be Detective Trudle. Third door on the left."

So down the hall and three doors later, he peered into an office with several officers. He recognized Uncle Johnny about the time he remembered that his last name was Trudle. He had just always been Uncle Johnny.

Johnny and Pat didn't have any children, so Andrew was their closest relative. He grabbed Andy and gave him his big ol' hug. For a moment, Andrew forgot why he came and enjoyed the moment. He and Johnny had always rough-housed around since as far back as he could remember.

Andrew then looked seriously at Johnny, "Can we talk?"

"Sure, come on in here." They entered his private office and found Crissy hard at work. "Andy, this is Christina. Christina, meet Andrew Roggerro."

They both did the nice-to-meet-you thing, but Andrew wanted a private visit with Johnny. "Could you excuse us for a few minutes?"

With a smile and a nod, Crissy was gone. Johnny began, "Hey, Andy, are you doing okay?"

His answer was simple and honest. "I don't know. This morning, Dad told me that he adopted me and that Uncle Joe is really my father." Now Andrew's emotions were all mixed up. His face began to go white.

Johnny saw it and had him take a seat. "What can I offer you to drink? And, no, I don't have any of that here."

"Coffee. Please. Jere just told me that everything Joe had was also in my name and that now I'm pretty well off ." Words came slowly for Andrew. His mind was operating on overload again, like your PC functions sometimes. There was just too much new data, life-altering data. His body was also medicating itself. His body would be fine, but it would just operate slower.

Johnny wasn't sure this was the right time, but there never had been a right time. "Andy, there's more. Joe's wife, your mother, was my sister, Marie."

One more surprise, "I hadn't put that together yet, but I like that surprise." A smile appeared.

Johnny was also smiling, now. "So tell me why you're here? You never come to visit me here anymore." Johnny handed Andrew the coffee and smiled as Andrew put five spoons of sugar in his coffee.

Andrew wasn't sure if he'd ever been here before. "I'm not sure, exactly. I was driving, and my Bug just sort of headed this way. I guess I wanted to know what you know about my father's death."

"Joe had just come in from DC. He had a friend that works at the Blue Ribbon. He had been trying to talk this young lady into changing professions. Just after she agreed to, he fell over and didn't wake up."

"Wait, you mean one of those girls out there was his girlfriend?" This was a real shocker. Joe was dating a slut or whatever!

Johnny could read Andrew's thoughts and tried to head them off. "Honestly, we think Joe had a girlfriend, but she's from DC. Micki is a dancer at the club. Joe went there with some friends one night and spotted her. She has dark auburn hair and deep blue eyes like your sister Erin. Erin would have been about Micki's age, and she and Joe just hit it off . She loved Joe because he didn't want anything from her except a smile."

"Well, have you talked to her? What'd she say?"

"Andy, the short answer is that I can't tell you anything except that I don't believe Joe's death was natural. I believe someone killed him. I can't tell you more because, because I don't want you in any more danger. These people killed your father, and I'm not taking any chances with you."

Andrew was so tired of people trying to protect him. "Now you're sounding like a cop and a lawyer all rolled into one. You don't sound like my uncle." With that, he turned and left.

Johnny just stood there, shaking his head. *If protecting Andy was the right thing to do, how come I feel so lousy right now?*

Andrew was talking to himself as he left the police station and hopped into his bug. *Why is everyone trying to protect me? Do they think I'm still a child? I'm twenty-seven now and I can take care of myself.* Andrew's head was throbbing again. There weren't any answers, just more and more information.

He was driving to Steve's house, but the Blue Ribbon Club and Micki occupied his mind. Steve and Andrew had been friends since kindergarten. They had both gone to St. Peter's College and had a great time while getting their degrees. Remembering some of the good things and good times with Steve had helped clear his mind, and for the first time, he noticed how heavy the traffic was.

Now home, Toll thought back about his visit. No policeman had been there. Everything seemed to be normal. Even Micki would be coming in later. Toll would have to visit it later as well. "PUG!"

Pug hated it when he did that. He didn't need to do that. But Pug knew he was a wimp and went to his master.

After Steve's graduation from high school, his parents moved about twenty miles away over to East Orange. Andrew had been there many times, but today, it seemed to take a lot longer. As Andrew was pulling up to Steve's parents' home, he noticed two very pretty ladies unloading some furniture from a U-Haul trailer. "Hey, don't the Donnatellis live here anymore?"

Carrie, Steve's younger sister, spoke, "Yes. They still live here, Andy. It's me, Carrie. This is my friend from school, Melissa Reems. Melissa, meet Andrew Roggerro of Jersey City and my brother's best friend."

Melissa wondered if people still believed in love at first sight. She instantly liked his smile, deep blue eyes, and that body. Acting very cool, she replied, "Hey Andrew. It's nice to meet you."

Andrew spoke to Melissa, but his eyes were fixed on Carrie. "Hey. What the heck are you guys doing?"

"Dad expanded my old room, and so me and Melissa are going to live there while we check out the job market. The school insisted that I leave my apartment just because I graduated. See if I ever graduate from there again." Carrie's moving clothes were skimpy, and she made sure Andrew noticed.

Still bothered by this very cute little sister that was suddenly not so little, Andrew tried to speak. "I, uh, came by to, uh, see, uh, Steve." He was very happy to finally get out a complete sentence. "Is he, uh, here?"

"No, but we expect him anytime." The truth was they had just arrived and had no idea where Steve was. "Why don't you help us until he shows?"

And actually, Andrew was in no hurry for Steve to show up. It was a good thing because Steve came home two hours later. The moving had worn Andrew out, but he was no longer stressed out. It was obvious that he hadn't paid much attention to Carrie these last several years. Somehow she had grown up under his nose.

He was looking at her again as she walked back into the kitchen and she knew it. For Andrew, the whole world seemed to stop. Carrie too just stood there, modeling here slender body. As if on cue, a gust of wind blew her silk blond hair, and she pivoted to see who was coming in from the porch. It was Steve.

Melissa was grateful for the reprieve. Now Steve would whisk Andrew off to safety. And she and Carrie Donn could get on with their unpacking. Melissa had seen Carrie work her spell before, only to dump the poor guy a week later.

Once more, Carrie flashed a smile, and her beautiful brown eyes winked. "Thanks for the help. I know Steve's going to steal you away."

Andrew could only say, "You're welcome."

Steve popped his bubble by grabbing him, and they wrestled around and did their ritual greeting. Steve gathered his own sandwich stuff and then settled down on the couch.

Now it was time to begin to explain how his life had changed so dramatically in the last twelve hours. "Steve, have you heard what happened?"

Steve hadn't heard yet. CDs don't broadcast any news, so Andrew filled him in. He told him everything that he knew.

For the time being, Andrew was going to live in the museum, but he hoped Steve would join him. "Say, Steve, what does Marcie think about Melissa moving into your house?"

Andrew's comments had the desired effects on Steve. His face turned into one big frown. "She really doesn't like it, man. She's really pissed. There's nothing I can do about it. This is my parents' place."

Again, Steve had made the correct response. "Why don't you move in with me? I can't stay in that big museum all by myself. Uncle Jere said that I shouldn't change anything right away."

As if fate were helping a little, the girls returned to the kitchen, passing through the den with a good bit of noise and bluster. Steve didn't have to think long. "So I can move in tomorrow if that's okay with you?"

Andrew was pleasantly surprised with the quick response. "It's a deal, brother. I'll let Mr. Silver know so that he can prepare a room for you. There's just one more thing. Are you busy tonight?"

"As a matter of fact, I am, Andy."

Well, he had gotten several right responses out of Steve. He had been hoping for one more. Andrew had wanted Steve to go with him, not that he needed anyone to go with him. Andrew had decided to visit the Blue Ribbon Club and look around. His head was feeling a lot better, but there were too many unanswered questions. Tonight, he would find some answers.

As it turned out, Steve lived just a few miles from 5 Dunbar Place. The traffic was really heavy, but finally, Andrew pulled into his new museum. He wasn't ready to call it home just yet. As Andrew walked up to the door, his instinct was to knock, but this was his museum now.

James opened the door as he approached. "Welcome home, Andrew." With a bewildering look on his face and waving his finger like a wand, he asked, "How do you do the door thing? You know. When someone pulls up. How do you know?"

"For security purposes, we have motion detectors, video coverage, and a buzzer goes off in my pocket. Sir, supper is ready. Where shall we serve you?"

Andrew liked the formality for about a minute and then he decided it had to go. "Can we talk to each other like normal people?"

"Certainly. Where, sir?"

"James, my friend Steve will be living here with me for a while."

"Will you be sharing the Master bedroom?"

"We're not that kind of friends, James. Give him a nice room. He's to have the run of the house. We both will be needing keys and the codes to the alarms."

James was startled with his last comments. "Sir, I don't understand. Why? I'm always here."

"Yes, and you will be, but just the same, keys and codes."

"Yes, sir."

Andrew was on a roll now. He might as well ask another question. "Is my uncle Jere here?"

"Yes, sir. He's in the study. He is almost finished with the official kinds of things that will need to happen."

"Thanks, James. That's where I'd like to eat and bring a plate for Uncle Jere." Andrew was not comfortable with the situation, but it was getting better.

CHAPTER

eanwhile, back at the Donnatellis' home, things were getting heated. One seldom wondered what Melissa was thinking because she would soon tell you. She had seen the look in Carrie Donn's eyes as Steve walked off with Andy, and she didn't like it. "Carrie Donn, Andy is too sweet a guy for you to pull any of your bullshit!" Melissa didn't mean to say it quite as loud as she did, but she meant business.

Carrie looked back at a Melissa she hadn't seen before. She appeared ready to do battle. Her face was flushed, and her stance was firm. Melissa had both of her fists clinched as if she were about to pounce. "What's the matter with you, girl? What'd I do?"

Melissa's face was flushed with anger and the thought that she might have a crush on the guy. "I saw the look in your eyes. He'll be another conquest of yours, and then you'll drop him. You can't pull that trick on Andy! He's the real thing. It was okay with those other clowns because they were only on a quest to score. But don't play with Andy!" Melissa surprised herself with her firm determination. She had stated her case well. She was waving her hands and using facial expressions trying to convince the jury.

The hair on the back of Carrie Donn's neck bristled. She liked a challenge. "Do I detect some competition? Go for him if you want to!"

Melissa was not about to back down on this. "Listen, it wasn't me he was drooling over, but just don't play with him. If you aren't interested in him, then don't lead him on. That's all I'm saying." Her heart was feeling much more, but nothing was ever going to come out of her mouth about it. Andy truly seemed like Mr. Perfect in so many ways. One little sigh did slip out.

Over at 5 Dunbar Place, Andrew had calmed down considerably. For the purposes of the funeral, he was willing to assume the role of Congressman Roggerro's son. This would be his gift to his uncle. Jere was willing to be the point person who would make all of the arrangements and set up all of the services and meetings. Andrew agreed with Jere that they would see if they could conduct the rosary and funeral at St. Peter's College. Their family members were all buried across the street at Holy Name Cemetery. The chapel was small, so the guests would be only family and close friends and those who needed to officially pay their last respects.

As Andrew and Jere visited, they realized that the numbers could grow, but those individuals would not be inside the small chapel. Speakers would have to be set up for those who might come without an invitation. The vice president had already called to say that the president would be coming back from Egypt in time for the funeral. He also indicated that he'd be bringing the speaker and a few others from the Hill. The governor had called and said that he would be attending also with a small delegation. He had agreed to activate three hundred guardsmen for the week to provide protection. With everything taking place at St. Peter's, there would be no long procession. People could come to the college and park and then leave. The internment would be private with only the family going into the cemetery.

Jere decided to combine his staff and Joe's staff with their two executive secretaries actually living in 5 Dunbar Place. Mary Bright was on a jet heading this way as they spoke. Jere needed his own, Fran Weekly. She had worked for him for twenty years and seemed to read his mind. He knew that if he gave her something to do that it would be done. Joe's office in the house could be converted into a control center. By keeping it in the house, it would be easy to make any necessary adjustments.

Andrew didn't enjoy large crowds, and the numbers kept growing. He decided that he'd be around them only when he had to. He had no interest in politics and all their games. He knew that they were coming to the funeral, but he just hoped they could leave the politics at home.

He and Jere had covered most of the details when Andrew decided he needed a break. "Jere, where's my dad's bedroom?"

"You've never been in there?"

"No way, that would have been totally weird."

"Okay, come on. I'll show you.

There trip was a short one. The office door connected to the master bedroom. Everywhere you could put a picture, there were photos of Andrew and Joe. Many of the pictures Andrew had forgotten about, but to Joe, they were his reason to keep serving his country. The photos were from games, fishing, graduations, and family picnics. Andrew was impressed. "I can't believe my eyes. Most of these pictures I don't even remember being taken."

"That's the way he wanted it. He didn't want to make a big deal out of it, but he needed these."

Andrew was overwhelmed. He truly had no idea. "I've got to go out for a while, Jere. Thanks for all that you're doing." He had hoped Jere hadn't seen the tears. Jere had seem them and acted like he hadn't.

He mounted his trusty gray Bug and headed out into the night. For the first week of June, it was still cool. The drive to the Blue Ribbon Club reminded him that it was not on the way home from the Newark Airport. Joe must have gone there for a reason. He could have gotten a drink even at the airport. Andrew decided he had to speak with this Micki.

Toll left about the same time that Andrew had, but he was much closer and arrived at the Blue Ribbon Club a few minutes ahead of Andrew. Toll intended to speak with Micki, even if it meant taking her for a ride. If she would talk there, then he would talk to her there. But if she wouldn't, then he had a plan B named Vinnie and Danny. They would be able to make her sing.

Toll was surprised at how busy the club was already. This time he'd have to sit more out in the open, and he didn't like that one bit. It sort of reminded him of the old West days, and he didn't want anyone behind him. At least, he could sit facing the door. His game would have to be played a little differently. He would really have to drink his drinks instead of pouring them out. His mind was no longer plugged into reality, but it was still very meticulous with a touch of genius. He could see step by step exactly what would need to happen tonight.

Andrew pulled into the parking lot of the Blue Ribbon Club and parked next to Toll's big blue limo. He had been to a couple of gentleman's clubs but not this one. As he walked in the front door, he was greeted with darkness and smoke. Like his father, he wondered how anyone could work here. Several people brushed up against him or bumped him as he made his way to the bar. "Hi. Can I get a Jack and Coke?"

Rosie's best friend was Micki, and she instantly knew this guy had to be the congressman's son. With a warm smile, she said, "Sure."

Andrew sipped on his drink as he tried to figure out a way to meet Micki. Girls wearing blue ribbons and fishnet came by, offering themselves to him for a price. As he continued to sip and ponder, he noticed the bartender exiting to the back. He would ask her about Micki when she returned.

Micki's thoughts were on what had happened about twenty hours earlier. She felt somehow responsible for the congressman's death. What could she have done differently, she wondered. One minute they were talking about her future plans, and the next, he's lying on the floor, dead. This would be her last night if she could even make it through one more. The congressman had loaned her fifty thousand to set up a small business, and she was going to do it. That settles it. "I'm leaving."

Rosie popped her head into the dressing area and called for Micki. "Hey, Micki. You're not going to believe this. There's a hunk out there that looks like a younger version of the congressman. I mean he's gotta be his son. But he don't have one?"

"Yes, he does!"

She made a quick dash to the bar, and there he was. Micki had never seen Andrew in the flesh, but she'd seen pictures of him, and there he was in the flesh. Even in the darkness, she could see the deep blue eyes, dark Italian hair with olive skin, and his father's firm chin. This was Joe's son. Micki was still holding her costume in her hand when she walked up to Andrew and said, "Hi, are you being taken care of?"

"Well, I have a drink. How do you get a table?"

"Someone like me will show you to a table."

"Do I know you?"

"No. But you look like someone I used to know."

"Do you work here?"

"I used to, but I quit tonight." She continued to lead him to a quieter section.

"You said that I looked like someone that you used to know. Can I ask who?"

Micki started talking as if she had known Andrew all her life. "A few years ago, Joe Roggerro came here with some guys. They drank and looked and had a good time. I waited on them, and Joe was really nice to me. A couple of nights later, he came back, alone. He requested a dance from me, but we just talked. My hair color and eyes had reminded him of his little girl's. She had died in a car accident a long time ago. Her name was Erin, and I guess she would have been about my age. So for the last couple of years, whenever he was in town, he'd stop by. He'd pay for a dance and we'd talk. Last night, he talked me into leaving this place. Just after he loaned me some money, I turned around, and he fell over. We were just talking." She had started crying as she began her story, but now she was sobbing.

Andrew did the gentleman thing and patted her back. In a moment, she hugged him and continued crying. Andrew felt uncomfortable, awkward, and good. He knew he was holding Micki, and he liked it. Yes, she was beautiful, but he liked being needed. "You know I'm Andrew?"

All she could do was nod.

"We need to get out of here. Okay?"

"In a minute." She had stopped crying, but she was exhausted.

Now that she wasn't crying, Andrew noticed her perfume, the texture of her long, flowing black hair. They sat there cheek to cheek. He started wiping her tears with his handkerchief. When he looked at her, he saw a beautiful lady, and he knew why his father had befriended her.

"Let me get my purse from the back. Can I just meet you outside?"

"Sure. I'll get my silver Bug."

Toll flipped out his cell phone and called Vinnie. "Plan B. She's leaving with her boyfriend. Wait. He's coming out first, so take him out and grab the girl. He's got a dark brown jacket and a yellow shirt with no tie. Not thirty yet with dark hair."

"We see him, boss. He's coming this way. What's the girl look like?"

"Five feet seven with long dark hair. She's wearing a pink blouse and a blue jeans skirt. Got some five-inch heels. I don't want you to kill the guy, just club him and take his money."

"We got it, boss. Bye."

In the back room, she couldn't get to her purse. "Hey, Nancy, can you hand me my purse?"

"What you got in here, girl?"

"Just some protection. If George asks about me, tell him I walked."

"Good for you, girl! I'm gonna, one day."

"Stay in touch." And she was gone. As she stepped out the front door of the club, she saw Andrew. Two men had Andrew. One was about to club him again. The other was going through his pockets.

With a scream and a shout, she caught their attention. "Noooo! Help!" She pulled out her protection as she was running toward them, firing as she ran. Her gun held nine rounds, and she fired nine rounds.

Andrew was dropped and the bad guys fled. She held Andrew in her arms, hoping he would be all right. "Keep breathing, Andrew!" Another Roggerro unconscious in her arms. This one would have to live. She would just will him to live. He had to live! She had to get Andrew over to Christ's Hospital.

George had been watching the activity on his floor when he saw Micki leaving on a night she was scheduled to work. She was his best dancer. She broke in the new hires. What would he do if she walked? He knew he should go after her, but it was better for her to go, so he watched. He followed her to the parking lot, and he called 911 on his cell. He covered her with his jacket and waited. She didn't even know he was there.

With a burning pain in his side, Vinnie threw down the club and ran away. "Hey, Danny. I'm gonna need some help here."

Without a word, Danny almost carried Vinnie to the car. No one was chasing them. The crowd seemed busy with the other guy, whoever he was.

"You gotta get me to the Doc, over in Queens. He can take care of me!" With that, Vinnie died. Danny got him into the car and drove slowly away, just another car out in Jersey City.

Toll's business was finished here, now. Danny would find out if she knew or suspected anything. Now he needed to leave and never return. An evil smirk appeared on his face as he thought about how easy it was to screw all these gullible people. They were all suckers just waiting for the right bait. He hated them all. None of them were on his level. They were all beneath him. Toll thought to himself, *I'll sleep like a baby tonight.* Then he walked outside. The flashing lights hurt his eyes for a moment, and then he watched Micki being helped inside the EMT vehicle. Her boyfriend was on a stretcher, and Vinnie and Danny were nowhere in sight. His laughter stopped, and vulgarities poured out of his mouth. After he noticed some people staring at him, he slipped through the crowd.

George saw him, but knew that he didn't want to see him or know him. It could cost a life—his.

Ron Dunn wasn't sure that he'd done the right thing by letting her ride with them to the hospital, but the patient was unconscious, and she knew him. She might be able to help with medical information and other stuff, plus she was really a looker. "Christ's ER, we're sending you vitals on a white male with head trauma. Copy?"

"We copy and are receiving data. Do you have an ID?"

"Miss?" Ron was looking right at Micki.

"He's Andrew Roggerro, the congressman's son."

"Holy Shit! Positive ID. We have Andrew Roggerro, the congressman's son. You're going to need to find Dr. Becker! We've started an IV. ETA is seven minutes."

CHAPTER

etective Trudle arrived just as Ron was closing the doors on the van, but he did get a glimpse of his Andy. And then he saw George Williams. He saw a man that was hiding something, but he wouldn't be hiding it for long. "Mr. Williams, so we called 911 two nights in a row. Life can be very exciting around here." People wanted to know what would happen with the owner, but they didn't want to be interviewed outside the Blue Ribbon Club, so most melted away.

Christi saw an out-of-control partner and she was worried. "Johnny, Bill and Al are here. Let's release this to them and go check on Andrew!"

Ignoring Christi, Johnny continued, "Isn't there something you want to tell me?"

George was getting worried, but he was still more afraid of those other guys.

"Detective, you must know that anyone that would go after a congressman and this other person wouldn't think twice about taking me out. I'm too old for all of this bullshit."

"This other person that was almost taken out, as you say, was Andrew Roggerro, the congressman's son." Then just loud enough for George to hear, he added, "And my nephew. If I find out that you're holding back any information that could put these people away, then

I'm coming back for you!" Now Johnny was losing it, and Christi knew it. She waved for Bill and Al to hurry over. "You might think that this is personal, but it goes way beyond personal. Also, if anything else happens to my nephew by these people, and I find out you were holding back information! You won't have to worry about your retirement!" Now Bill and Al were pulling him away from George Williams.

Bill was really angry, "Christi, if you don't get him out of here, I'm going to arrest him. Tell him he's off this case and the congressman's. When I talk to the chief, he'll be lucky if he has a job."

Johnny had been acting some and not acting. He had wanted to scare Mr. Williams into telling what he knew. The bad guys could use guns. All Johnny could use were words. Words, this time, he had meant.

George Williams didn't know who to fear most, the crazed detective or Toll. George wouldn't be sleeping until he figured it out. In his pocket, he found the officer's card with his name and phone number. He didn't even know that it had been put there.

Detectives Walden and Wilson questioned those still there and didn't find out much. Their main report would be on the behavior of soon-to-be former Detective Trudle.

Danny drove into a quiet commercial section of the Queens. One honk and a garage door opened. Dr. Sam knew his customer and knew there was trouble. Dr. Sam was a vet, but he could treat people if he had to. "What do we have here?"

"It's better for you not to know. He just needs to go away." Then Danny helped the doc get Vinnie out of the car and into the incinerator."

"Tell Toll not to send me any more business. He's too hot. You need to burn that car as well."

"It's next." With that, Vinnie became part of New York's smog problem. The car would have a similar fate.

The paper had sent Bo Houston to the club to sniff out anything that hadn't been told about the death of the congressman. "Hey, Mark, I ran into the congressman's son, tonight."

"Bo, you've been there too long with too many drinks. We all know that the congressman's wife and daughter were killed in a car accident twenty-seven years ago. The man is single and nearly a saint. He doesn't have any children!"

"I just heard Detective Trudle threaten the owner of the club, saying that was his nephew and the congressman's son. His sister was married to the congressman. I'd believe him. His son's name is Andrew, Andrew Roggerro."

"Okay, Bo. I'll do some more checking. If Andrew Roggerro is admitted to the hospital, then we've got a story! I'll let Lynn know."

Doctors Becker and Schloop were working in the ER when the call came in from Ron Dunn. When the doors to the van opened, Dr. Becker was looking at his second Roggerro in less than twenty-four hours. Officially, this was Nick's son, but he and a few other people knew that Nick had adopted his nephew.

Ron spoke before Dr. Becker could, "He appears to have been hit twice on the head with a club of some sort. He's stable, but he's going to have a big headache when he wakes up."

"Good job, Ron. When are you heading off to med school?"

"Got turned down, doc. I'm staying right here."

"I'll see what I can do. I still have a few contacts there. Rachel, let's get an MRI on Mr. Roggerro." Then Dr. Becker noticed Micki. Her hand was holding Andrew's, and she didn't appear willing to let go. "You know, miss, you will have to let go of him when we do the MRI." He smiled at the shocked young lady.

The doc had been trying to joke with her, but she didn't change her expression. She just nodded. "Miss, he'll be okay. I just want to verify that we don't have too much bleeding. If we do, we can deal with it, but Andrew will be okay." Morris was saying that for her benefit, but it was mostly true. They should be able to take care of Andrew now that he was in his hands.

Rachel had spent the last ten years of her life in college, med school, interning, and now a resident. She hadn't had time for men in her life, but this was the prettiest man she had ever seen. He was taken obviously, but this was good motivation for her to get back out there and start having a life again, whatever that means. "Miss, what's your name?"

"Oh, uh, I'm Micki, uh, Michelle Phillips." Micki had been deep in thought, hoping that her almost brother would be okay.

"Andrew, I'm Rachel Schloop, your doctor. Micki and I are going to take you over to another room and do an MRI to see how much damage was done to your head. Micki's going to keep holding your hand except while we do the imaging. Is that okay with you?" Rachel always told her patients what she was up to. If they were awake, then they would want to know. She would want to know.

Andrew was somewhere between awake and out there in la-la land. His eyes weren't focusing, but Rachel's voice was nice and soothing, and he also knew that Micki was still with him. Andrew tried to say okay but his body didn't carry out his request. Next he tried squeezing Micki's hand.

"Oh! He just squeezed my hand twice. I didn't realize that he was awake."

"You never know." Rachel smiled and walked a little straighter.

"Andrew, I'm sorry this happened to you tonight, but I won't leave your side until you fully wake up. Okay?" Two more squeezes. Looking at Rachel, she said, "He did it again."

"That's a good sign. He's with us. It's kind of like infants who can't speak yet but can understand. They can sign before they can speak."

The noise of the ER faded as he closed his office door. Once again he would call his friend Nick with bad news. He wondered if he'd been working in the ER for too long. He dialed Nick's number one more time.

The phones had already been switched so that they were routed to 5 Dunbar Place. "Roggerros, Fran speaking. How may I help you?" Fran

Weekly was at work and would live here until after the funeral. She was more than a secretary. She was a friend, a sounding board, a helper, a complete person; and she worked for Jere.

"Yes, this is Morris Becker from the ER at Christ's Hospital. I need to speak with Nick or Ellen."

"Certainly, Dr. Becker. I'll patch you into his cell phone. We've routed all calls through 5 Dunbar Place. One moment, please."

"Hello, this is Nick."

"Good evening, Nick."

"Oh, hi, Morris. Did you find out anything yet on Joe?"

"No. We sent off a sample of his heart and liver over to a special lab to run a couple more tests, but everything looks like he had a heart attack. The reason that I'm calling is that I have Andrew over here. He's been hurt, but he appears to be okay."

Nick's heart was in his stomach. "What do you mean appears to be. Can't you tell?"

Morris was about to lie for his friend so that he wouldn't have an accident on the way over to the hospital. "He's a bit groggy. He was mugged over at the Blue Ribbon Club. I guess he went over to see if he could find out any additional information. Come on down and check on him. His friend Micki's with him, so he's not alone. We're doing an MRI on him right now to make sure there's no excessive bleeding. All of his vitals are okay.

The next hour was uneventful. Rachel got to know more about Micki Phillips. The MRI proved that everything was okay. Rachel had given him some pain medicine that should make him sleep until morning. And Micki was still holding his hand as promised. Micki had a chair right next to the bed and could lean on the mattress.

When Nick and Ellen arrived, they were met by Dr. Becker. He escorted them to Andrew's room. "Your Micki won't let go of Andrew. We made her let go during the MRI, but she's been with him the whole time."

Nick knew of Micki, but he didn't know her name. "Morris, we've never met Micki. This is the first we've heard of her."

The lamp was lit next to the bed. It lit up Micki's face as if a holy aura was surrounding her. Ellen said, "Look, he's got his own guardian angel."

Nick was more serious. His son was in the hospital, and Ellen was making jokes. Micki started to rise when they entered the room, but Ellen told her not to. "Keep your seat, dear. We just needed to look at him."

"He's much better now. Drs. Schloop and Becker have taken good care of him. He's resting well."

Morris liked the compliment. "Thanks, dear. Do you need anything? Can we get you something?"

"Thank you. I'm fine."

Before Nick could ask any questions, Ellen whisked him out. "He seems to be doing good, dear. We'll see you tomorrow."

Micki was surprised but nodded and smiled. They hadn't asked who she was, and she didn't have to explain anything. Then she looked back at her patient, and they left.

"Ellen, I was about to ask who she was!"

"I know, that's why I got you out of there. They needed to be alone." Her smile said that she recognized Micki, but Nick hadn't. "Okay, so who is she?"

"His big sister, Erin. That's who Joe's been going to see. Andrew must have found out her name. I don't know how much they talked, but I guess they were leaving together."

"Oh my goodness! Well, let's go home."

In the locker area of the Jersey City Police Station, a sad and dejected Johnny Trudle wondered about many things. Had he to do it over again, would he talk the same way to Mr. Williams?? Sure he would. The guy is a creep.

Christi finally found him. "Hey what's up?" She knew, but she needed to let him tell her. If he'd only come when she had said come.

But isn't that the trouble with most men, they never listen to that woman's voice of reason?

"The chief said that I was to take a week off . If I showed my mug around this place before that, then I would be fired."

"He can state things clearly sometimes. And me?"

"He said that he'd hook you up with a new partner tomorrow. I was to stay away from you. If I call you, then you get a week's vacation also."

"So absolutely don't call me here at the station. You'll have to use my cell phone." She smiled and he laughed. She could do that to him.

"Well, I guess with all my free time, I'll go check on Andrew. I hope he's talking to me."

"What happened between you two?"

"I told him to let me handle this because I didn't want him getting hurt."

"Duh!"

Danny had checked in with Pug because Toll wasn't around. Pug paid off Danny and told him to go and find another job. If he stayed around here, Toll might kill him. They both knew Toll, so Danny hit the road. "Danny, call in a couple of minutes, and I'll let the machine get it. You can leave a message and tell Toll what you told me. Then throw your phone out the window of your car."

Pug knew he needed a distraction. They were also called ladies of the night.

Johnny ran into Nick and Ellen in the ER with Dr. Becker. "So how's Andy?"

Nick could smile now. "I think he's in good hands. Micki's up there with him, and he's resting."

"Micki. I need to talk to her."

Ellen grabbed his arm and said, "That can wait till tomorrow. They need some time alone. And I'm going to buy you a drink at my favorite place."

Johnny saw a determined woman, so he agreed. "Where're we going?"

"Home."

Nick phoned Jere and told him that Andrew was doing okay and, unless something happened overnight, he'd be released the next day. That started a chain of calls. Jere in turn called James Silver so that he could make preparations for having Andrew picked up. Steve was to be told etc.

CHAPTER

Fr. Jason O'Raley had heard about the attack on his old friend's son, so he made sure that Andrew's was one of the rooms that he visited on his morning's rounds. He would be saying three Masses today, but not until later. Right now, he was concerned about Andrew.

Fears are often fueled by the unknown. So there was a deep, long sigh when he saw Andrew resting comfortably. A smile appeared on his face when he noticed the peaceful young lady resting her head next to Andrew's. She seemed to be very content and happy in her task of watching over her friend. Father Jason chose not to disturb their sleep but said a prayer for both.

He started to leave, but his last glance of Andrew reminded him of a young Joe Roggerro. It had been almost thirty years ago that they had been buddies. For Joe, life was full of fun. For Jason, life was full of pain. He lived vicariously through Joe. Joe was his reason for not dying. Joe was full of ideas and dreams about how great this country could be, and he thought he could make a difference. Joe ran for Congress and won, and Jason followed him to DC. Then the unthinkable happened. Erin and Marie died in an accident because Joe wouldn't cave in and take a bribe on some pork-barrel legislation.

Jason remembered how angry he had become. He was even angry at Joe because Joe wouldn't just lay down and die! "How can you act like this! You just lost your wife and daughter!"

"Jason, I got very angry for two days, but then, at their funeral, I told God thank you for the time that I had with them."

"What about an eye for an eye?"

"At the funeral, I was able to leave that up to God."

I remember I was so mad at him for all of the crap he was spouting. Those evil individuals who killed his family could not kill his faith or his love of his country. He would serve his country, but he had Nick adopt Andrew for safekeeping.

It wasn't long after that conversation that Jason started attending church with Joe. Once involved in church, Jason found God's calling for his life. If Joe had given up, so would have Jason. Jason knew that he was alive today because of Joe Roggerro. He wondered how many other lives Joe had touched. Quietly, Jason slipped out of the room, going on to check on others in need of some hope and a prayer.

A while later, Andrew's stirring woke Micki. He looked around and recalled the previous night's activities. In a voice that started as a whisper, he asked, "Micki, are you okay?"

"Yes."

Andrew's vision was slightly blurred and his head ached; otherwise, he felt pretty good. "There was a guy hitting me and then there was an explosion. He dropped me and ran. I think someone may have shot him. Do you know what happened?"

"Andrew, when I came out of the club, I saw a man getting ready to strike you again. I screamed, but he didn't let you go, so I shot him. He dropped you and ran. I waited with you until the EMT people came, and I made them take me as well."

"So you saved my life?"

With a smile on her face and pride in her heart, she said, "I'm no heroine, Andrew. I keep that gun for my protection. It was only a reaction. I think my boss, George, called 911."

"Have you been here all night?" Andrew couldn't understand why she would have stayed. He didn't know her, and she didn't know him. But he was glad that someone was there. She was pretty, nice, and pleasant to talk to.

"Yes. I wanted to make sure that you were okay. I owe it to your father. Besides, I wanted to make sure that you were okay for me, too. I don't have any family, so I didn't want to lose you. I don't know what I'm saying. I mean your father thought of me as your sister, and so you were the closest thing that I have to family. Jeez, this sounds so corny."

Micki began gathering her stuff so that she could leave. "Listen, you're okay now, so I'll just head on out. Okay?" What Micki was really thinking was that she was trash and that no respectable person would want a stripper hanging around. Her eyes were filling as reality set in.

Andrew reached out and took her hand. "Can you stay a little longer? I want to talk some more, but this room won't stop spinning. I need to close my eyes." Not long after his eyes were closed, he was sleeping.

Once again, she laid her head down next to Andrew's, but she didn't go to sleep right away. Her mind drifted here and there, from now to last night, too many nights ago when she had been left alone by a family that had left her behind. One of her foster parents had called her a princess, but she knew that her mother would have never left her if she had been a princess.

Life was full of surprises. She liked the warmth of being next to someone who just wanted to be with her. Now those happy thoughts allowed her to drift off .

Outside their room, life was changing. The Sunday-morning shift had arrived and was getting briefed. Myrtle O'Tool, the new charge nurse, had been a nurse for thirty-five years. Having Andrew on her floor added a little spice to life on her ward, and she liked a little spice now and then. A plainclothes policeman was replaced by one in a uniform. The only one not to come by yet was the doctor. He made his rounds on his schedule and not the floor's schedule.

Across town, Tim arrived at Steve's house to pick him up and some of his things. Steve drove a yellow Mustang convertible, but not today. He would pick it up later. It wasn't big enough to take everything that he wanted. On his way out the door, he told Carrie, "See you later. Oh by the way, you know that Andrew got mugged last night and spent the night in the hospital. I'm picking him up later this afternoon."

Carrie wasn't awake yet, and so the data came in kind of twisted. "Melissa, did you hear what Steve said?"

"I think Andrew is in the hospital."

"Dad, did you hear what Steve said?"

"Yes, dear, Andrew's over at Christ's Hospital. He was checking out the club where his uncle had his heart attack. Steve said someone tried to rob him and he wound up in the hospital overnight."

"Melissa, if you're going with me you'd better hurry up because I'm almost out the door."

"Don't you dare leave without me, girl."

Almost out the door meant another twenty-five minutes, but that was still pretty fast to look "normal" for a girl. They ran down the steps and out the door. Neither spoke on the way to the hospital. By ten, they were quickly walking up to Andrew's room as if nothing had been done for him all night and they were the only ones who could take care of his needs. Their pace slowed as they saw the long dark hair and then the face of a very pretty lady who just happened to be holding their Andy's hand.

Micki had seen jealous eyes before and decided to be nice before they could be mean. "Hi. Are you friends of Andrew?"

Melissa spoke for Carrie, "Yes, we are." It was almost a challenge. Micki was not going to play any games this morning. She ignored the challenge and just started talking about Andrew. "He's had a long night, but he's better. He took some water about an hour ago, but mostly he's been sleeping."

Just then Steve walked in, followed by a mean-looking nurse. "Hi, ladies." Steve knew that Micki would be there, but she didn't look anything like he had expected. She was beautiful, soft, tender, gentle, and all those other words that make you fall in love except he was already engaged.

Before anyone could say anything, Myrtle called them outside. "Do you see that nice man sitting over there?" Pointing to the policeman, "If you're not on his list, then you can't go in there."

Steve answered, "I know I'm on the list, but he's not awake so I'll check on him later." With that Steve left Carrie and Melissa with Myrtle.

"You're not old enough to be his mother and that's the only other female on the list. Bye, Darlings."

Officer Gonzalez had been watching and was having a good laugh. "All right, ladies, you'll need to leave now. He should be released later on today."

"You think it's funny that I have to do your job, do ya?"

The answer was yes, but Officer Gonzalez knew better than to reply.

Carrie and Melissa walked out, crushed. Not only could they not take care of Andy, but some other person was there, holding his hand.

As the drugs and alcohol wore off, Toll noticed something cold next to him. It hadn't been a bad dream. He had killed the prostitute. Her crime had been that she couldn't arouse him in his condition. Toll was losing more of his mind as each hour passed. His insanity was fully in charge. To Toll, she deserved to die. No crime had been committed on his part.

Pug heard his name along with a few other words, so he reported to his boss. He tried not to act surprised when he saw the dead hooker. Surprise would buy him death as well. "What do you need, boss?"

"I know what you're thinking, but she was trash. She had a miserable life. I simply put her out of misery. Get rid of her." Toll was too busy to help. He had to take a shower.

Pug decided that the girl could stay in bed. He was not going to become an accessory to this senseless murder. On his way out of Jersey City, he planned to stop by to see if Gail or Sharon or both wanted to split with him. He had a nest egg and one of the trucks was in his name, so he could leave on a moment's notice. This seemed like the right moment.

Somewhere in Newark, in a very private office, a man said, "Hey, Lucio, I don't want anything else to happen to Joe's boy. Am I clear?"

"You want me to cap him, Mr. Marcus?"

"Not yet. If they leave him alone, no. Send Marty down to talk with this Tolbert fellow. Maybe he'll listen, but probably he won't."

Micki was getting worried that Andrew had been forgotten about. The ward doctor with his students had passed right by the room, and no one had been by since. She was about to go and find Nurse O'Tool when Dr. Schloop came in.

Dr. Becker and Dr. Schloop had spent the night in the hospital. Dr. Becker had said he would go and check on Andrew, but Rachel insisted on seeing him. It had nothing to do with him being the prettiest man she'd ever seen. She just wanted to follow up on her responsibilities. "Good morning. How are you two doing?"

"Fine. He's been sleeping pretty much the whole time."

"That was my intent. He needed to be still and rest." Her touch on Andrew's shoulder woke him."

"Is it still morning?"

"For a few more minutes. I'm Rachel Schloop. I greeted you last night, but you might not remember. You've been hit on the head pretty hard. There's still some swelling, but you should be able to go home in a couple of hours. No driving and just move slowly. Your vision will return to normal in a few hours. Wear sunglasses when you go outside because it will seem brighter. You're still very sensitive to the elements. Don't turn or move your head quickly, and in a few days the headaches will stop. Take this for your headaches every four hours. Any questions?"

"Do you have a card, doc? And thanks."

Now, speaking to Micki, she said, "I expect you to remember what I just said because he's still too groggy to remember."

"I'll take care of him." Then Micki was alone again. Andrew smiled and then closed his eyes.

Toll came out of the shower and called for Pug, but Pug didn't respond. He was on his way out of New Jersey. He'd called Sharon and Gail, and they both agreed to leave with him. Toll didn't know where his number one was, but he had better have a good reason for not being here or else he would be having serious health problems.

Toll had forgotten about the hooker until he saw her still lying on the bed. He went out into the garage area and found Mike and Angel. "Mike, get in here."

"Okay, boss."

"Have you seen Pug?"

"He seemed in a big hurry to go somewhere, boss. He took the red rig. Said he'd be back soon."

"Well, he killed this hooker last night. I told him to get rid of her. I think he might be trying to steal my truck and leave town."

"He was in a big hurry, boss, but he's not stealing that rig 'cause it's his. That red rig is his. I saw the registration one time, and it was in his name. He told me not to say nothin' to nobody 'cause you'd get mad if anyone found out you gave it to him."

"Jesus Christ, does anyone around here have their heads and brains connected? Mark, you and Angel get rid of this body right now. I don't want to know where, but take it out of state."

"Yes, boss. And you don't have to worry about me. I'm not having any headaches. When I do, I just take two aspirin. You want I should get you two aspirin, boss?"

Toll never heard him. He was out the door and on his way to Sharon's place. She'd been his girlfriend for a long time now. But he hadn't seen her in the last couple of weeks. He didn't know what to say to her anymore. She wanted a wedding, and he wanted her gone. As he left, he told himself, *I'm gonna kill that SOB!*

By 2:00 p.m. at 5 Dunbar Place, Mary and Fran, with a few workers from their respective offices, had taken over the library and were taking care of a mountain of problems. Jere was making his wishes known, and they were handling the details.

Mary Bright's bags were still packed and lying on a bed somewhere in the house. She had come in on a noon flight to Newark. Within a few minutes, she had started in on her task of handling all of the people issues. If it involved people, she was to handle it.

Special Agent Judy Snap of the Secret Service would be occupying Mary's time for the next several hours. They needed to cover everything that the president would be expected to say and do. Presidents only ad lib if they want to get into trouble. What they say is always said before they say it to see if there could be any problems. A small committee works on everything the president says. Agent Judy Snap was working on expectations and security. Her team would check out routes, locations, and structures.

"We sent a message through the VP's office that the president wanted five minutes during the service. Is there a problem with that?"

"Miss Fran and Jere are working on the service, but I'm sure that won't be a problem."

"Ms. Bright, I also asked for a windshield tour of the area. My team needs to check it out."

"I'm Mary. And Peter Roggerro, the congressman's nephew, will show you the campus and the chapel where we'll hold the rosary and the funeral. Just let me know when you're ready to roll." Mary was involved in a Christian church there in the DC area. She could do anything in the service, but usually she ran the service, tying everything together. It was Mary who had contacted Natalie Cole and Andre to see if they would sing at the funeral. They would be there.

"What about the priest doing the service? Can I meet with him?"

"I'm sure you can, but you'll have to call his office and check on a good time. He works everywhere, but he's assigned to St. Joseph's. Those guys work about sixteen hours a day. There should be one hour in there when he can see you."

Meanwhile, Fran Weekly was busy taking care of all of the logistics. Flowers and donations would be coming in in huge quantities. Jere even trusted her to finish the funeral arrangements. He did suggest a cherrywood casket. Fr. Jason O'Raley would be conducting both the rosary and the funeral, with Fr. Mario Cente helping in case Fr. Jason had any troubles completing his best friend's services. Both services would be by invitation only. For the funeral, there would be speakers outside for those who wanted to attend. Inside, there would be one camera that would feed the funeral service to all the media.

Nick's Comiso Bakery would be shut down for the next week. The Roggerro family had enough to do without worrying about the shop. Pete and Mike had tried unsuccessfully to talk their father into keeping it open.

Nick had few relatives in America. Most of his cousins still lived in Comiso, Sicily. They were far from the political city of Rome, but Rome's new policies and partnerships were completely unacceptable to his father, Giovanni. Just before WWII broke out, Giovanni gathered his new bride and all their savings and came to America. The Roggerros were not the only Italians fleeing their homeland. It seemed they were coming by the thousands.

Ellis Island was not a fun place, but when they would get discouraged, they would just look over at Lady Liberty. The statue seemed to be calling them. When they came ashore in Jersey City, they stopped. Here, Giovanni and Estella would start a bakery and help other Italian Americans get settled. During the war, tensions ran high, but that didn't stop them from buying Giovanni's bread. There were thousands of Italian Americans in Jersey City, but all of the different ethnic groups loved his bread. Nick and Joe had continued helping folks. Ellis Island was only a tourist stop today, but new immigrants were still settling in Jersey City. And they still love Nick's bread.

Many of their old friends would want to attend the rosary, and this was okay. Nick would host a dinner for them before the rosary there at 5 Dunbar Place. The funeral would need to include a number of dignitaries. The chapel could hold almost three hundred, but they expected several hundred would be outside. Joe loved St. Peter's College and really wanted to use their chapel for his funeral. The vice president had asked Nick to bring the funeral to Washington, but Nick declined. They would make do in Jersey City.

Myrtle O' Tool had come on duty at seven and was now sick and tired of the steady flow of people that were trying to see her patient. So she posted a sign: "No Visitors."

Seeing the sign, Johnny Trudle considered it a speed bump in the road of life. He simply spun around and sought out its author. "I'm Detective Trudle, and I'm looking for Nurse O' Tool."

"I'm Ms. O' Tool, officer. How can I help you?"

"I'll just be needing to speak with Andrew."

"Not until he's released this afternoon." After her answer, she walked away.

"Ms. O' Tool, I need to talk with him now, if you don't mind!"

"I do mind, and you won't be, officer. Whatever you need doesn't come before his rest."

"Nurse! If you'll just point me to his bed, I'll be about my business."

"Officer Trudle, I believe, even though you haven't shown me any identification, I don't come down to the police station telling you how to do your business, and you won't be telling me how to do mine!"

"Maybe I need to speak to the doctor on duty here."

"Sure, let me call her." Ms. O' Tool kept smiling the whole time, knowing what Dr. Schloop would say. "Dr. Schloop, Detective Trudle wants to ignore the No Visitors sign you had me post on Mr. Roggerro's door."

"Let me speak with Detective Trudle." She handed the phone over to Johnny.

"Hello, doctor. I'm sorry to bother you, but Ms. O' Tool won't let me ask Andrew a few questions about what happened. And I need to get on with my investigation."

"Sir, Ms. O' Tool is following my instructions. You can talk with our patient after he's released. That should be later this afternoon. Thank you and good-bye."

Johnny wasn't used to being thwarted. He didn't say anything else. He just left.

Myrtle gave the uniformed officer a glare like *I could have used some help here.* But he knew she could handle it. She turned away from him so he wouldn't see her laugh. It would blow her mean-gal act. Men can be so dumb sometimes. I wonder how those single guys get by without a woman telling them how to get things done.

Nurse O' Tool heard one of those damn buzzers go off. Somebody wants to know if they can go potty. Or *Ma'am, do you think I'll go home soon?* After being on your feet for seven hours, they get *damn* attached to them. It's too close to the sound that a dryer makes when it goes off. Well, Nicole can get this one. "Nicole, can you just answer one of those without me having to tell you?"

"Huh, are you talking to me?"

"Nicki, who else do you see around here?"

"Well, uh, ma'am, can you take this call from Governor Cardetti?"

"Give me that phone, girl, and go check on that room."

"This is Ms. O' Tool."

"And I'm Richard Cardetti. I understand that you have Andrew Roggerro there? May I please speak with him?"

"Sir, we don't get many calls from the governor, if this is the governor. He's still resting, but I could let you speak with his friend Micki. Please stand by while I transfer your call." Nurse O' Tool passed the call on to Andrew's room, warning Micki of who would be on the other end. "Just be yourself. He's just a man."

"Hello, this is Micki."

"Hi. This is Richard Cardetti. I was just calling to check on Andrew's condition. How serious are his injuries?"

"Sir, he was being hit on the head with a club when I came out of the club. I screamed and then shot the guy. He dropped Andrew and ran away. There were two of them. Right now Andrew's sleeping, but he looks much better. I think they are about to release him to go home."

"Can I ask what you and Andrew were doing at that place?"

"Well, sir, I used to work there. Andrew's father talked me into quitting, right before he had his heart attack. Andrew just wanted to hear more about what happened. He was going outside to get his car, and I went back in for my purse. That's when he was attacked."

"Wait a minute, don't you mean Andrew's uncle?"

"That's kind of a long story, sir. But Joe is Andrew's birth father and Nick adopted him. They were afraid something like this might happen."

"Well, this certainly is a surprise. Listen, I've spoken with Mr. Durbin, and he knows that I'll be down for both services. Would you pass that information on to Andrew for me? Also, tell him he's in our prayers. Bye now. I look forward to meeting you."

"Thank you, sir, and I'll give him your message." I just spoke to the governor of New Jersey, oh my God!

Meanwhile, over at 5 Dunbar Place, it seemed like Grand Central Station. Jere had been in contact with several VIPs. The governor would be attending both the rosary and funeral while the president would only be attending his friend's funeral. They would caravan over from Newark and go directly to St. Peter's Chapel. Then they would leave as quickly as possible. From Newark, the president would head back to the White House.

The governor would be more difficult and easier at the same time. He would drop in for dinner and the rosary and then leave. Then he will also join the family at the chapel for the funeral. His plans are to rough it at the Hilton.

Steve was also now living at 5 Dunbar Place. For now, he was just waiting on Andrew to call for a ride home. He was amazed at the size of his new home but more impressed with everything going on. For the next couple of days, he was willing to do whatever Andrew needed him to. Tim found Steve and told him that Andrew had called and they were releasing him, so they needed to leave.

Tonight, Beth and her additional helpers were preparing a meal for fifty. Each night that number would double. Tomorrow, as many as one hundred guests from the old neighborhood would be coming and then going to the rosary. Italians greave in their own special way, but privately. The media would not understand, so there would be no media at the rosary. On Tuesday, a smaller number from the Italian community would be able to go inside the chapel because of the many dignitaries, so tomorrow would be for the Italian community.

As Steve and Tim were leaving, Peter and Special Agent Snap were just returning from her tour. She had to have her plan completed tonight so that enough agents could be deployed to protect the president. Normally, they have months to prepare, but you have to be able to react to emergency situations like this one from time to time.

Over at Christ's Hospital, Dr. Schloop had released Andrew. With a sparkle in his eye, he surprised Micki with a proposal. "Let me run something by you. As of today, you're unemployed. In the future, you hope to start your own business. Let me hire you as an aide or secretary for a couple of months, and that will allow you to not rush into any busy dealings overnight. Then, when you're ready, you can open your shop."

"Andrew, what would I do? Do you need a secretary?"

"I don't know what I have, so I don't know what I need. I mean my father left me everything, basically. But I have no idea what. You can help me sort it all out. He has a staff, but they are already busy on other stuff, so you could work with me directly."

"Okay, but let's not talk about any of the details right now."

"Okay, except for one. I'd like you to move into our guest house for now so that you are close. It's going to take a lot of sorting out in the beginning."

If anyone but Andrew had made her this offer, she would have slapped his face and walked out. It sounds like he wants a mistress, but she'll trust Andrew until he proves otherwise. "Andrew, I'm renting a sleeping room from my friend Verna. We'll need to drop by and pick up a few things before we go over to the guest house. It's amazing how much one's life can change in a day."

"Tell me about it. When Steve and Tim get here, we'll swing by and have Steve pick up my Bug and meet us at home. Then we can have Tim take us by your place."

"I have one thing as well. I need to buy some "aide" clothes. Most of what I own would not fall under that label. I can get started on that tomorrow."

"I can have Tim take you, and I'll pay for the clothes."

"I should have been working for you before." They both laughed. She wheeled the chair over to his bed, and he easily rotated into the chair.

Nurse O' Tool had clocked out, but she was willing to help the staff coming on the floor by escorting Mr. Roggerro to the front door. "Come on, Mr. Roggerro. Let's get you out of here. You're a big troublemaker. Not really, but you sure did keep things interesting around here today."

"Thank you, Ms. O'Tool. Glad to do my part." With that, they were off to the main entrance and a waiting limo.

Nurse O' Tool had one parting shot. "If I didn't have my car here, I'd ask for a lift. Nice car."

"Tell everyone again thanks for everything." Andrew was on his feet for the first time in a while. He let Tim hold the door this time. Micki slid in beside him, and he took her hand. Tim was in lust as he looked across at one of the most beautiful sights he had ever seen. Micki didn't look down. She was used to those eyes.

"Tim and Steve, I'd like you to meet Micki. She's coming to work for me. For the next few weeks, I'm going to have her stay in the guest house." Steve obviously liked that idea. He wanted to see as much of this lady as he could. Now she would be living next door.

"Andy, you didn't tell me you had a new girlfriend."

"I wouldn't classify her as a new girlfriend. I'd just call her a friend. Tim, would you call James and ask him to be sure that the guest house is ready?"

"Certainly, sir."

"Do you have to call me *sir*?"

"Certainly, Andrew."

"Thanks, Tim." Both men smiled at their understanding.

Over at Steve's place, the house was fairly quiet except for two brooding ladies. Carrie asked Melissa, "Have I played with guys at school?"

Melissa couldn't believe that she was hearing these words from Carrie's mouth. "How many guys did you date? 'Let me count the dates.'"

"That's 'Let me count the ways that I love you.' Come on, Mel, I'm trying to be serious."

"Yeah, I know, and I can't believe it. You dated, but you were never serious with any of them."

"I know why now. I've been in love with Andy since I was ten."

"You sure couldn't tell yesterday."

"Zing. Okay, I played with him yesterday. I've been dreaming about him for fourteen years, and he finally gives me some attention. It was harmless. Do you know that I used to dress up in my mother's clothes and play like we were dating? The guy thought that I was a lamp in the house until yesterday. And now, someone else is holding his hand and comforting him. Aughhhhhhhh!"

"CD, how is your brother getting around town?"

"Mel, I'm pouring out my heart and soul, and you are wondering about my brother's transportation situation! He was picked up in a limo for goodness sakes! Aughhhhhhhhhhhhhhh!"

"I mean, do you think he'll have need of his Mustang? We're not too busy. We could be nice sisters and drop it off. Maybe we could stay for supper. Miss 'Whatshername' might be gone, and you could pick up where we left off, with him drooling all over himself."

"We haven't left yet! You're so good to me, Mel. You can be in my wedding."

"Wait a minute. Tonight, we're just going for a little drooling. He's a hard nut to crack. It might be a day or two before he proposes."

"Okay, I can wait a day or two." Then the preparation started. To look like "normal" takes thirty minutes. Looking "special" takes an hour or more, so they just went for the "normal" look, and then they were off to do their good deed.

Toll returned to what he thought was an empty office. He hadn't been able to find Pug, Sharon, or Gail. *If they all have cut out, I'll kill 'em. They can't desert me and not pay for it.* Just then, he noticed a light on in the back office. *If they're here, I'll still kill 'em. I can't have people around that I have to worry about all the time.*

His insanity was interrupted by a soft, firm voice from the shadows of his office. "Hello, Mr. Tolbert."

"Who the hell are you, and what are you doing in my place?"

"It doesn't matter who I am so long as you see that I'm holding my friend Millie, as in Nine Millie."

"We don't keep any money here. I have nothing to give you."

"What I need, you have. I need you to give me your word that you'll leave the congressman's son alone."

"The congressman doesn't have any family. They died in an auto accident a long time ago."

"Your people mugged Andrew Roggerro last night and nearly killed him. If you bother him again, I've been instructed to erase you from the game of life."

"If I don't give my word?"

"Then I'll do it now."

"Who's your boss?"

"You're not in a position to ask questions. Yes or no?" Marty cocked the nine mil for emphasis.

"I can leave him alone."

"We are done talking. If you ever see me again, I'll be sending you to hell."

CHAPTER

Steve headed toward 5 Dunbar Place with Andrew's gray Beetle. Meanwhile, Tim was heading over to Verna's house so Micki could pick up a few things until she could decide where she wanted to live. Verna managed a Walmart at the local mall. When Micki and Andrew arrived, Verna was nowhere around. Tim stayed in the car so he could check his eyelids for any holes.

"Andrew, could you give me a few minutes to shower?"

"Sure, I'll call the house and tell them that we'll be there in a little while."

Andrew was ready to find a place to sit. He was okay but just unsure of doing too much too soon. After his call to 5 Dunbar Place, he found a Walmart catalog and began checking it out.

Micki was floating on air as she went into her bedroom. Then she stopped dead. On her bed was one of her old Blue Ribbon costumes. It could be unsnapped and completely removed. Her past was always going to come up. She knew that she would have to dance for Andrew before she could work for him.

Andrew was surprised by the robed Micki. He had expected it to take a lot longer. "That was quick."

"I haven't had a shower yet. Andrew, I used to work in a sleazy business. We made money off lust. You need to know what I used to do for a living." With that, her robe came off and she started her dance music.

Actually, Andrew had gone to a gentleman's club before, but Micki was right in front of him. The music was loud and the beat strong. She had a lot of natural rhythm, but Andrew wasn't thinking about that. His face flushed, and his body was responding to her gyrations. What had lasted ten minutes seemed like an instant to Andrew. He knew his lust alarm was sounding.

She stood before him with nothing on. Her body dripping with sweat. Her breathing was rapid, but she just stood there. Andrew was her captive. He sat unable to move and not wanting to move. If she came to him, they would make love. No, they would have sex, but not love. He wanted her to stay, and he wanted her to leave.

Micki stood there, looking at him. If he motioned for her to come to him, she would. They would have sex, and then he would have to leave. She would not be able to work for him. She wanted to be his friend, not his lover. She could not refuse him. Her debt to his father was too great, so she waited.

For Andrew, the silence was deafening. Her long dark hair shimmered and her body glistened. She didn't smile or look angry. She looked at him and he at her. He thought she was beautiful. If the dance had seemed like an instant, her stillness seemed like an eternity.

And then, she swooped up her robe and walked into her bedroom and then into the shower. She was floating again. She thought, *He's like his father. I'm so glad that there are people like them out there.*

She was still smiling when she came out of her bedroom with a suitcase and a makeup case. She walked as though the suitcase was empty, and she was floating on air.

Andrew noticed, "Micki, you look like the cat that ate the canary."

"Oh, I'm just happy. What'd you think of my routine?"

"I didn't know I could get that sexually aroused without having sex." She grew serious for a moment. Setting the suitcase, she took his hand,

"Andrew, we could have."

Andrew didn't know where she was going with her comment, so he asked. "Is that what you wanted?"

"No, but I needed to show you what I've been doing for the last eight years. Your family and friends aren't going to like you being around me, a stripper." She held her head down and didn't look at him. She couldn't bear to look at him.

He took his free hand and placed it under her chin. Then he raised her eyes to meet his. "I'm not sure if my father, Nick, knew about you. Probably, Uncle Jere knew about you. And who knows who else."

She could look at him again. "Your father's girlfriend knew about me." Andrew's eyes widened, "Which father, Joe or Nick?"

"Joe, of course."

"Whew. I'm glad it was Joe. But none of us knew about her."

"Her name is Suzy Waggoner, and she's from the DC area. That's all I know."

"See, Micki, you're already helping me with my father's stuff . There's a Ms. Waggoner working for Mary Bright. She has long blond hair and is about five-five."

"That's gotta be her. I think Joe was about to pop the big question to her."

"Wow, after all these years too. Listen, we need to hit the road, lady." He took the suitcase, and they headed to the limo.

Back at 5 Dunbar Place, James opened the door to find several people arriving at the same time. "Good evening, Mrs. Durbin, and is this Danielle?"

"Yes, James. It's so good to see you. Has it been a little busy around here?"

"Madame, if it were any busier around here, we'd need a traffic officer. Do come in. Everyone is gathering in the formal dining room."

"Thank you, James."

"Good evening, Mrs. Roggerro and Mike. How are you doing?"

Ellen responded, "We are fine, James. I'm just sorry that we are over here because of what has happened."

"Yes, ma'am. It was quite terrible. Ma'am, everyone is gathering in the formal dining room."

As James was about to close the door, a gray Beetle pulled up as did a yellow Mustang and Melissa's red Explorer. Steve spoke to the girls, "What are you guys doing here?"

Carrie cooled her brother's heels. "Do we have to talk about this out here?"

James greeted them. "Please come in. Everyone is gathering in the formal dining room. Follow me, please."

Steve tried to say that the girls weren't staying, "Uh, I don't think the girls want to stay for supper."

Melissa responded, "Sure, we do." Carrie handed her brother his keys. The girls were following like they were on a tour. "Mel, Andy's got a butler."

"Carrie, this place is so big we have to have a tour guide to show us were the café is." Both girls giggled with that.

Carrie had been looking for Andy but hadn't seen him yet. "Hey, Steve, where's Andy?"

"He and Micki were going over to her place to pick up a few things. I think she's going to be working for him. Andy thought she might like to live in the guest house for a while. You know, to see how things work out."

This was the worst possible news for Carrie, and Melissa was upset as well. Steve didn't have a clue that Carrie was interested in Andy. He was like a big brother to her, so he thought.

"I assume that Micki was the lady at the hospital. Who is she?"

"Well, until yesterday, she worked at the club where the congressman died. Andy was mugged just after he met her. They were heading out the door to go somewhere else to talk about what had happened, but he was attacked."

Melissa was incredulous. "You mean that Andy has hired a stripper to work full-time for him? Why, she's probably dancing for him right now. Then into the sack for a quickie and then home for supper and then maybe some dessert later."

Steve was not going to put up with Melissa's behavior, "Melissa, you need to lower you voice. Any or all of what you said may be true. But you are my guest in his house, and I will not allow you to act this way. Settle down, or there's the front door."

"Well! I most certainly will! Come on, Carrie, let's leave." And she started off .

Carrie was quiet but not moving. She feared the worst but hoped for the best. "Mel, I'm staying." One more time Mel had flown off the handle and expected Carrie to fly with her. It hurt Carrie not to go, but she needed to not jump at conclusions. Like Steve said, it might all be true, but she hoped to find out from Andrew.

James followed Melissa out but held the door for her. She wouldn't be able to slam it. She just kept walking with her head held like a charging bull.

The dinner was just about to start when Carrie and Steve walked in. Nick was standing and about to offer a toast. They were seated and then Nick continued, "A toast to Joe, my brother and friend." There was a moment of silence, and then Nick offered another toast. "I want to thank each of you here tonight for what you have done already and what you will do in the next few days."

Micki and Andrew walked in arm in arm. He had been a little unsteady on his feet, and he liked holding on to Micki. He could almost imagine an older sister for the first time in his life, and it was nice. Andrew made a swing around the room, saying hellos to all. He didn't introduce Micki to anybody except his parents. They smiled and greeted her with Ellen kissing her cheek.

While Ellen distracted Micki for a moment, Nick told Andrew what had been on his mind all day. "Andrew, Joe probably is not here today because of his legislation fighting organized crime. If they knew that you were his son, they might have gone after you as well. It probably wasn't a second random act of violence at the same place."

Andrew didn't want to think about it tonight. He just wanted to enjoy his family and friends. "Dad, if I can interrupt you for a second. Let's let Johnny do his work and stay out of his way. Tonight, let's remember Uncle Joe and enjoy each other's company."

"That's a deal, son."

Micki had taken a seat about four people over from her. Andrew sat down beside Micki and only waved to her and Steve. Nick called on a priest to offer Grace. Then the priest started moving around to the other tables, shaking hands with everyone. He even knew her and Steve, but he didn't know the evil thoughts she was thinking about Micki.

Then Jason introduced himself to Micki. "So you're Micki? Joe said that he was going to back your new business if you'd let him. I guess we'll never know how that adventure would have worked out."

They were just far enough away that Carrie could only make out every fourth or fifth word. Then Micki spoke, "I don't know. You might. He loaned me some money just before he passed out. I was so happy, and then the worst possible thing that could happen, happened."

"I looked in on you and Andrew this morning. You make a great couple. I hope we see a lot of you."

"Father, listen. Andrew proposed something to me, and I accepted. He wants me to work for him during this time of transition. Then I can take my time switching to something else. I'll not be in any hurry."

Carrie could only hear parts of their conversation, but she heard, "great couple," "proposed," "accepted," and "be around." That told her everything she needed to know. If she had ever had a chance with Andrew, she let it get away yesterday. Now there wasn't any room left. She slipped out of the dining room and walked toward the door. She was going home, somehow.

James saw her coming and played like he'd never seen those kinds of tears before. "Are you leaving, miss?"

She nodded.

"May I have Tim drive you?"

She nodded again.

He raised his cell phone and asked Tim to bring the limo around. "This way, Ms. Donnatelli."

She looked up sharply. She didn't know that he knew who she was. When she looked up, she revealed how much she had already been crying.

She didn't want or need this house and these things that now belonged to Andrew. She only wanted Andrew. Now she only wanted to leave.

Tim opened the door for her, and James told Tim that she was Steve's sister. "Make sure she gets home safe, and go slowly." Tim had no idea what he was talking about, but he would get her home safely and slowly.

When Andrew noticed that Carrie hadn't come back, he asked Steve, "Where's Carrie?"

"Don't know. She was here just a moment ago. I thought she went to the ladies' room."

Andrew went down the hall, looking for her and ran into James. "James, have you seen Carrie?"

"Why yes, Andrew. As a matter of fact, she was very upset. Like her heart had just been broken."

"That would be me. I'm not sure what I did, but I did something."

"Yes, I suppose you did."

"What are you talking about?"

"I think she came here to see you, but she couldn't get close to you. You know, Micki."

"Oh, she thinks I like Micki. Where is she, James? I can straighten this out."

"Not so fast, Andrew, Tim is taking her home."

"We need Tim to turn around. This is real important to me, James."

"One moment, sir." Again with the cell phone, he said, "Tim, turn around and come back and pick up Master Andrew. He wants to escort Ms. Donnatelli home. Turn slowly so she doesn't realize what you are doing."

Andrew figured out why Carrie had left. He remembered the words she may have heard, and they didn't sound good. She was in love with him and thought that he was in love with Micki. Carrie hadn't noticed the phone call or the turns. The limo stopped, and the door opened.

Andrew knew she didn't want to see him right now, so he acted for her. "Hiya, dollface."

She thought she was home. She didn't want to see him right now. Her heart was breaking, and he was the reason. "Get out and leave me alone!"

Okay. He'd have to try something else. "If we're going to get married, then we've got to work on our communication skills and trust."

"Will you just leave me alone? You're not funny."

"I'm not trying to be funny now."

"Andrew Roggerro, stop teasing me. I heard her say you proposed to her and she accepted and that she's moving in."

Carrie was more rational and a little less emotional than she had been. So Andrew tried to explain the words that she heard. "See. This is what I'm talking about. Where's the trust? I proposed that she come and work for me, and she accepted the position. She's moving into the guest house because I asked her to. Her place is way over on the other side of town." Andrew chanced getting into the limo.

On the intercom, Tim asked, "Where to?" Andrew replied, "Take her home, please."

Carrie's tears had stopped, but her face was wet and her eyes red. Meekly, she said, "Well, Mel said that she probably danced for you at her place."

In a soft and loving voice, he replied, "I'd have to say she did."

Carrie couldn't look at him now. She asked the next question anyway. "Mel said that you probably hit the sack next." Who could blame him? She is so pretty. Ohhh.

Again softly, he replied, "We didn't."

This wasn't the answer that she was expecting. How could he not have? "Am I supposed to believe you?"

"One word, *trust*."

"Why would a skilled stripper dance for you in her home and not be willing to have sex with you?"

"She said that she wanted me to see what she had done for a living. And, yes, she was willing to have sex with me, and I could have had sex with her. But I'm not in love with her. I'm in love with you."

All she could say was "Oh."

Andrew felt pretty good now, so he asked, "Is this when we kiss and make up?"

"No kiss. There's been enough near sex tonight. Just hold me."

"I'd settle for that."

They embraced, and she cried some more. "Now what did I do?"

"Nothing. I'm just happy. I thought I lost you tonight. I've been in love with you since I was ten. That's a long time."

Both needed to be held. And both liked who was doing the holding. This time, Tim drove all the way to Carrie's home. Andrew didn't want to let her go, but he needed to get home and get some rest. His head was really hurting again. So with great reluctance, he left her at her door.

CHAPTER

Tim had been watching TV in the front of the limo when they announced that they were about to break away for a special news bulletin. Just then, Andrew returned from walking Carrie to the door. Without asking Andrew, Tim turned on the TV in the rear of the limo, thinking there might be news about his father.

"We interrupt this program for a News 4 bulletin. Here is Mike Shantz."

"Thank you and good evening from Channel 4 News. Tonight, the nation is still mourning the death of our own native son, Congressman Joseph J. Roggerro. He died of a heart attack at a local bar just after midnight on Saturday morning. Channel 4 News has been told that he was returning from the Hill. He stopped by for a drink and to visit one of the employees. Our sources have also told us that the congressman had befriended one of the young ladies there and stopped by from time to time. His purpose was to get her to change professions. When we tried to interview the young dancer, we were told she had quit. Maybe he was finally successful in that regard."

"Also, even though the coroner claimed the cause of death was due to a heart attack, local police Detective Johnny Trudle has said that it is still under investigation. This means that foul play has not been entirely ruled out."

"Let's go live to Sean Risen at St. Peter's College."

"Good evening, Mike. It's quiet out here tonight. But starting tomorrow, this place will have as many policemen as City Hall can spare along with a large number of National Guardsmen called up just for this week. Tomorrow at 6:00 p.m., Father Jason O'Raley will begin conducting a rosary service for the Roggerro family and some of their close friends. We've been told that the governor will be in attendance, but don't try to come. You must have an invitation from the family in order to get in."

"Then on Tuesday morning at 10:00 a.m., President Ashcroft and a small delegation from the Hill will join the governor and attend the funeral. Mike, in order to attend the funeral, you guessed it, you must be invited by the Roggerro family. Bishop Dan Moore has limited the number of guests that can come inside the chapel, but the family has agreed to set up loud speakers outside for those without invitations."

"The Secret Service people are already here, working with the Roggerro family on the president's visit. Following the service, he will leave, and then only the family will go into the cemetery for the internment. He will be laid to rest next to his wife and daughter, Marie and Erin, and his parents, Giovanni and Estella Roggerro."

Giovanni, or John as he liked to be called, and his new bride immigrated to America right before the war. They set up a bakery and never looked back. Joe was not the people's first choice for congressman. They tried to draft Giovanni, but he said that his place was here at the bakery in Jersey City. Then Joe said he would like to run and has been there ever since."

"Sean, have you heard anything about the president requesting that the funeral take place in Washington?"

"My sources confirm that, but the family has remained steadfast. They say that Joe stipulated that he wanted his funeral to take place in Jersey City. The family's spokesman is a local attorney and friend, Jere Durbin. He said that he politely turned down the offer. Congressman Roggerro's public life will end here in his hometown. With Channel 4 News, I'm Sean Risen reporting live from St. Peter's College."

Andrew sat there for a moment, and then he looked up seemingly at the roof of the limo and began to pray. "How do I pray? Is it saying what's on my mind? I have so many things on my mind, God.

"How could you let my family die? Why am I left? How am I going to get to know my other father? I have found out some things about him, but there is so much that I'd like to know.

"What was so important that you had to keep him from me? I feel so cheated! So guilty! I want to know about my other mother and sister as well. They're all gone now!" Andrew finished his first real prayer, and then he cried. He cried for his father, mother, and sister. Now his grief focused on his other family and not himself. The center of his universe was changing. Where there had been anger, there came a kind of peace that passes all human understanding. He was still sad over his losses, but he was at peace.

Carrie was also on his mind. Dropping her off hadn't been easy. He was going to have to get some sleep. Tomorrow was going to be one long, tough day.

When Andrew arrived back home, the older generation was still in the game room, sitting around talking and remembering things about Joe and Marie. Andrew just sat and listened. Maybe, he thought, some of his questions were going to get answered tonight. His brothers and a few other young people had separated and moved out to the patio. Something told Andrew that he was in the right room. And, for the next two hours, he heard more about his other family than ever before.

Finally, Demri told everyone that she was taking her man home for at least a few hours of rest in his own bed. There was a mutual agreement by all that it was time to turn in. The young people left a little later, allowing Andrew to get some sleep.

Beth was glad to have some people in the house, but this was ridiculous. Many of the twelve bedrooms were in use. The library and office were constantly full of people. One couldn't walk around the house without running into guests. She was trying to figure out whom she would need to feed and what to feed them. Tim had taken Andrew's friend Steve and the new girl into New York for some shopping, so they wouldn't be needing anything. Mary and Fran had indicated that they would just have a continental breakfast, so she multiplied that by five and set up a buffet. Demri made Jere go home last night, but he would be over before long and he was going to want biscuits and gravy. Beth made a note to make some extra in case others wanted some as well. She didn't know what the young Mr. Roggerro would want, but he was going to need a good breakfast. He was in for a long day.

Many things were going on behind the scenes. The Secret Service were in town and scoping out St. Peter's College. The governor had sent his sister, Rita Woodhead, to make all of his arrangements. Mary was off checking with Bishop Moore and the facilities at St. Peter's. Fran was working on the final few who would join the list attending supper and the rosary.

Teresa Jackson had been keeping an eye on her late husband's business and did not like the looks of things. She decided that she would start at the top and clean house. She found the main office basically trashed. She called a temporary employment agency and asked for three workers. They would need to be flexible, very flexible.

Next, she phoned Mr. Tolbert and told him not to come back. He didn't say much, but he certainly was not happy. She told him that if he came around, she would have him arrested for trespassing. Her next call was to the police station, saying that she was afraid of Mr. Tolbert.

Then she began to clean up Tolbert's mess. She called Gary Boggs, her personal banker, and told him that she was taking charge of her company and that she had fired Mr. Tolbert. He was not to have access to the accounts any longer. When asked about the thirty-five different credit cards, she said to cancel all of them.

Mrs. Jackson set into motion a chain of events that she could never have imagined. When she cut off the credit cards, the fifteen trucks out on the road were stuck. They had been operating on credit, and now it had stopped. Also, down in southern Mexico, another credit card was rejected. Milo and Jack had to come up with money of their own to clear their account. Toll was not answering his phone, nor were any of the guys at the office. By the time they got around to trying their cell phones, they had been cut off as well. Teresa had been a busy lady this morning. She would get busier.

Toll had been blindsided by Jackson. He would take care of her later, but for now, he needed access to his funds. As of this moment, he was out of money. Most of the money in the account was not his. When Jackson found out whose it was, she would have to release it to him, or they would come for him and her. His mind told him that Roggerro was the cause of all this. Well, the congressman could only die once, but that rogue son of his would pay for this.

Over at the Donnatelli house, two young ladies were stirring. Carrie had been up for a few minutes and decided that her news was too good to keep any longer. "It didn't work again."

"Carrie, don't play games with me. I just woke up. What didn't work?"

"The beauty sleep, silly. You're still the same, Mel." She laughed for the first time in a few days, and it felt good. Then wham she was struck by a flying pillow.

"Mel, how'd you do that? You didn't even open your eyes."

"What's for breakfast?"

"Melissa, you always eat cereal and drink milk."

"No, sometimes Dad makes me waffles 'cause he likes me better than you."

"Mel, we're not really sisters. You're just living in our house, wearing my clothes, and eating our food."

"That sounds like I'm family. Hey, you're not crying. So how'd it go?"

"Well, let's see. He said something like if we were going to get married, then we have a lot of work to do in communication skills. Then we hugged, and we didn't talk much after that."

"What about the stripper? Are you gonna let her hang out at his place?"

"That was something else that he said. He said that I was going to have to trust him a little bit."

"Who was it that said something like 'Trust, but verify'?"

"Mel, you can be vicious even before breakfast."

"I can do a lot of things before I open my eyes. I wake up ready to fire." Melissa was glad to have her friend laughing again. When they found Micki in Andrew's room, holding his hand, Carrie had thought that Micki was his girlfriend. She had been devastated. She hadn't cried; rather, she just closed out the world. It was like being around the living dead. That magical sparkle in her eyes had disappeared, and a cloud of unhappiness cloaked her. If your best friend hurts that deeply, then it's ones responsibility to help change the situation. Melissa wasn't sure that she had helped, but at least she had tried.

Their friendship started back in elementary school. They called each other's parents *Mom* and *Dad*. Some thought that they were identical twins. Neither family had a great deal of money, so the girls frequently exchanged clothes. This exchanging never carried over to their boyfriends, but many times they each had little crushes on the other's boyfriend.

If Carrie decided that Andrew was not right for her, Melissa would go after him faster than a dog chasing a meat truck. Andrew had all the qualities that she was looking for in her man. But Carrie would have to reject him first. She would not come between them. Plus, his younger brother, Mike, looked pretty hot last night. That was the first time that she had seen him dressed up, and he cleaned up pretty good. Mike's friend Chad looked pretty hot too. Melissa thought to herself, *Life is good*!

Meanwhile, a couple of miles down the road, Andrew was just getting out of bed. He had gotten eight hours of sleep, but he was still tired.

Dr. Rachel Schloop had said that he would have a dull headache for a few days, and she was right. He really didn't want to face everyone and everything just yet, so he called down for Beth to send him some coffee and bagels.

Andrew was amazed at the size of his home. He was in a guest bedroom, but it was the largest bedroom he'd ever slept in. He doubted that he would stay in the house past the one year that he had promised Jere. Joe may have liked big, but Andrew liked to know where things were. He didn't want to have to ask someone else to get him this or that, although this morning it was nice. Yes, those things would change, but later. Right now, he needed to get through the next couple of days.

He liked having Micki around. Her eyes reminded him of a puppy. At first, they were sad, but when she thought that she could be like a sister to him, they filled with joy. He knew that she loved him like a brother. She was a neat person, but he wasn't thinking of her as a sister, just yet. For him, she was an employee. If they had fooled around at her place, then he wouldn't have been able to keep her close to him. His mind would have been on other things. He was not sure why they hadn't fooled around. Everything had been perfect except for love. Still, what kept them apart? Life gives some answers, but it seems to be better at leaving us with more unanswered questions.

For Micki, this was all special. She had been looking for a family all her life. Joe had started coming by a couple of years ago, but he had stayed at a distance until recently. Then he offered her enough money to get started in something else. But now he was gone. When Andrew came along, it was as though God had given her another chance to do something useful and fulfilling with her life. When she was around Andrew, it was like she had hope through him. She felt like he was so pure and good that she was better just by holding on to him or by being around him.

Yesterday had been the best day of Micki's life. She hoped that it would continue into today. Steve was a big help, but she also knew that he was just in lust with her. It was okay. He was behaving himself, but his eyes treated her as if she were a China doll that might break. She no longer was in the business of trying to lure people with her body. Now she wanted to impress them with who she was. For, right now, she was Andrew's assistant; and that's how she needed to dress. It would probably be several hours before she and Steve finished this awful shopping.

Andrew had just slipped on a pair of shorts and a T-shirt when someone knocked on the door. "Mr. Roggerro, I have your breakfast."

"Come in please." He was glad that Suzy had brought the tray up. "Thank you, Suzy. And my name is just Andrew."

Suzy was surprised that Andrew had remembered her name. She had almost become his stepmother. But that secret died with Joe. "You remembered my name, Andrew. I'm flattered."

As he took the tray from her, he said, "My close friends have always called me Andy. I'm sure that a stepmother is close enough to qualify as a close friend." He liked surprising people, and it worked this time.

She was almost speechless. She stammered, "How'd you . . . Nobody knew." Then she had to sit down.

"Your secret's safe with me—that is, as safe as you want it to be. If you want, we can let it be known that you were engaged to Joe, or we can keep it a secret. Tonight and tomorrow, though, I want you to be in the family section with me."

When she looked at Andrew, she knew where his kindness came from. She reached over and hugged her stepson. She stayed a little while and then left to get back to her tasks. "I need to stay busy, but I'll sit with you tonight and tomorrow. And thanks."

Andrew needed a shower to wake him up the rest of the way. The hot shower reminded him of his hurt knee and his shower Saturday morning. Life was still changing rapidly. He now had a stepmom, girlfriend, and a new sister. He had been playing at life and having a great time. Now it was time to accept his adult responsibilities. The irony of the situation was that he was really ready to take them on. He wished that somehow the circumstances could have been different. Still, he was willing to play the cards in his hand.

At that moment, Andrew had one more visitor at the door. Johnny Trudle hadn't been to Joe's place in a long time. He felt a little uncomfortable ringing the doorbell at his brother-in-law's home. Now, Marie, Joe, and Erin were all gone, murdered by thugs—thugs who thought they couldn't be caught by the law, thugs who didn't bother following the law except when it worked in their favor. Johnny also believed they were thugs that he could and would catch one way or another.

James greeted him, "Good morning, Detective Trudle. Please come in."

"Thanks, James. I stopped by to see Andy before it gets really busy around here."

"Sir, I can't begin to tell you how busy we've been around here. Please, help yourself to some coffee. I'll tell Andrew that you're here."

When she picked up the phone, Fran said, "Andrew, Johnny is here to see you."

Andrew had just stepped out of the shower, but he wanted to talk with his uncle. "Fran, could you send him to my room?"

"Sure, Andrew."

"Thanks." Today was starting off like Andrew had thought it might. These next couple of days could be the busiest of his life thus far.

He had just enough time to slip on some clothes before Johnny came in. "Hey, nephew. How's it going?"

"Actually, a lot better than I thought that it could've when I was in your office. I apologize for acting the way I did. A lot of things had happened before I got to your office. I just didn't know what to do. People that I would do anything for seemed to be keeping things from me, and it made me very angry."

"Yeah. A lot of things seemed to hit the fan when Joe died. We didn't know what to do or how to handle it. It just all came out. I don't have a good answer for you. Know that we love you and we're just trying to protect you. I guess we kind of bungled it.

"Let me change subjects, Andy. I need to ask you a few questions about Saturday night."

"Okay, but I'm ready to get out of this bedroom. Let's go to the library. No, the pool."

Andrew and Johnny found the pool area to be empty for the time being. He told Johnny as much of what had happened as he could remember. Parts of it were blurred, and other parts were simply not there. Johnny became very angry at the thought of almost losing his nephew.

"Andy, what do you know about your mother's death?"

"I know that my father was threatened, and apparently it was carried out on my mother."

"That's basically it. I traced everything back to Jackson Trucking, but I didn't have enough hard evidence for the police to arrest the owner. Ironically, about five years ago, his brakes failed on him, and he died in a vehicle accident. Then again, maybe someone is still causing accidents.

Johnny looked down for a moment. There was a tear in his eye. "I miss your mom. She was my best friend. Our parents seemed to be on another planet, but Marie was always there for me. And I let her down by not sending that SOB to the chamber. Little Erin was so sharp. That little cutie had Joe wrapped around her little finger. He would have done anything for her, but you can't uncrash a car."

"Why do you think Joe's death was caused by someone?"

"Your father died when his heart stopped working. I think someone put something into his drink at the club. He was just about to get some very damaging legislation passed to help track dirty money. Organized crime couldn't have been very happy with his bill. I also think that they tried to kill you because they think that you might take your father's place on the Hill."

"This is pretty weird, Johnny. You've seen too many movies. I'm not going to take his place. I'm going to run his businesses. I wouldn't know the first thing about being a congressman."

"Let me say this once, and then we can drop it. You have the governor of New Jersey coming to your home today and the president will be at the funeral tomorrow. That's a lot of political punch. You don't have to know much. It's all in the timing, plus you have name recognition. Did you know that your dad and the governor were good friends? I'll bet that the governor will ask you into a private room to speak with you alone. Then he will tell you that your country needs you to carry on your father's work. He is the governor, and he'll have your attention. You'll try to say no, but he'll take it as a yes. Then the next thing ya know, he's announcing that you're considering filling in the remainder of your father's term."

James Silver interrupted their visit by announcing that Father Jason was here to see Andrew. Johnny excused himself, promising that he and Pat would be at the rosary.

Andrew stood up as Father Jason O'Raley entered the pool area. He didn't dress like a priest, but Andrew recognized him. But he didn't know him. Up until this week, church hadn't been very important to him. Now that death had entered his life, he had begun looking closer at things that he used to keep at arm's length. "Hello, father. You know I have a real good excuse for missing church yesterday."

"Yes, I heard that you'd been out to a strip club or something." Jason had a big grin on his face as Andrew was embarrassed by his teasing.

"I've not come to hear your confession, son. I just wanted to see how you were doing. It's good that you've a sense of humor in the midst of all that's been going on. By the way, how's your prayer life?" Jason smiled as he asked because he felt he knew the answer.

"How'd you know that?"

"Know what?"

"That I said my first prayer in a while last night?"

"That's why I'm here. When people lose a family member or have a close brush with death, they start thinking about God. So I'm here to answer your questions."

"Excuse me, but this is really weird. I mean another weird thing. God told you to come here this morning?"

"Yes and no. No, he didn't tell me over the phone. I just felt that I needed to come by. Now what are your questions?"

Even though he was talking to a priest, Andrew felt comfortable. So he jumped on the opportunity to find out about some of the things that he had spinning around in his head. "Why did God take my family?"

"My understanding was that someone on earth sent them to heaven. They were murdered by someone here."

"Yeah, but God could have stopped them."

"Yes. He could've stopped them. But he didn't. We are his instruments. Why do we allow people to do this?"

"Father, was it something I did?"

"No, Andy. Nor was it anything that your family did. Joe was doing what God had called him to do, and that was to serve in Congress. He was a great congressman and a great person. He helped so many people. Joe was willing to loan Micki money to get her out of the club business. Who do you think suggested to President Ashcroft that he ought to run for president? Your father's faith kept me alive until I found my own. When people were around Joe, they fed off of his faith, happiness, and peace. I'm trying to say that he attracted people, and when they left, they were better off . Our world needs a few more like your father."

"How come I never knew any of this?"

"Joe served his country, and it cost him his wife and daughter. He was still willing to serve his country, but he wasn't willing to lose you. You were the most important thing in the world to him. Frankly, I told him to quit, to give up. That next Sunday after the funeral, I went to church with him and found his source of strength."

"He asked Nick if he and Ellen would adopt you, and then he returned to the Hill. I quit as his aide and enrolled in seminary. I wanted to help others the way I had been helped and strengthened. The night Joe took me to Mass, I thought that he was crazy, but I went with him because I didn't want to be alone. He didn't go to church for himself but rather for me. I really didn't understand what was going on in the service, but I found myself praying. I mean really praying for the first time, and then I started crying. It was as though God heard my plea and released all that I had been carrying for so very long. After the service, I felt a peace I had never known."

"Father, some of this I did last night." Andrew felt relieved, finally being able to tell someone.

"I know. I can see it in your face. You're at peace. You have lots of questions, but you are at peace."

"Damn, how do you do that? Uh, I'm sorry. I didn't mean to say that."

"Andy, I need to leave, but I would like to pray with you first."

"Okay." Andrew thought, *Why not? It could only help.*

"Jason placed his right hand on Andrew's head and, with his left, held both of his hands. Then he began. "Heavenly Father, I thank you for the Roggerro family, for those that are in heaven and those still here. I pray that you will have your angels surround this one and protect him. Help him through these next few days as I know how hard they will be. Continue to use him, Lord. I pray that he will do your will here and that you will bless him and his service. I pray this prayer in the name of the Father, Son, and Holy Ghost. Amen."

Andrew didn't look up as Jason left. He sat there motionless for a few moments. He felt at peace. Something had happened to him during that prayer. Not anything from the outside but rather something from within.

Just before noon, Billy Ray Tolbert strolled into Jackson Trucking with a couple of goons. They found Teresa Jackson in Toll's old office, trying to place a 911 call for help. She was so frightened that she collapsed. Toll just let her fall. He was angry, and he wanted her to feel pain. But he needed her alive for now.

"Boys, put Mrs. Jackson on the couch. I'm gonna say this once, lady. It's your trucking company, but I had put some of my money into the account, and I need it back. And some of that money belongs to some very bad people who will do more than just walk in here and ask for it back. They will blow this place up and you with it. So, lady, just transfer my $5,500,000 to this account," and he handed her the number, KjKiv57869Q , "by 4:00 p.m., or I'll tell 'em that you refused to do it. Your little girl will lose both parents. Ya know that I killed your husband. He was gonna get rid of me. What else could I do? Four o'clock today, lady!"

Toll and his goons left as quickly as they had come. On their way out the door, they trashed the front office area. The police tape recorder couldn't pick up that noise, but it did pick up what transpired in Toll's office.

When the police arrived, the last of the temps took off . Teresa Jackson had not moved from the couch. Ron Dunn's EMT team wound up taking her to Christ's Hospital where Dr. Schloop had her admitted for observation.

Johnny had heard that there was a problem at Jackson's Trucking. He called Christi on her cell to find out what had gone down. "Hi, lady. Miss me?"

"How ya doin,' Johnny?"

"Pretty good. Can you tell me about the call from the trucking company?"

"Yeah, Johnny. But not over this phone and not now. I'm actually working this one as we speak. Call me after your gathering tonight."

"That's not the answer I'd like. But deal!"

Steve and Micki responded normally to inner city traffic. They blamed each other for choosing the Lincoln Tunnel instead of using the Holland Tunnel. Tim could tell they were arguing about the traffic and laughed to himself. When he looked back again, they had stopped arguing and were locked in each other's arms. What had started out as a day of shopping had suddenly become complicated. He tried not to look in his rearview mirror, but he had to. His instructions had been to swing by Steve's house to pick up a few more items. So he decided to head there.

Micki felt passion for the first time in several years. She had become so used to acting on stage that she wasn't sure if she could feel it again. Steve had been treating her as if she were a china doll. Then the argument happened, and then they were kissing. Her desire for him was overwhelming her. She knew that his passion for her was just as strong. If they had been someplace private, she would have wanted more. Her mind was racing. She kept telling herself that she couldn't get involved with Steve, and now she couldn't let go of him.

Tim purposely jerked the limo when he stopped so that the lovebirds would know that they needed to let go. It worked. They tried to straighten their clothes as though nothing had happened. Micki decided to stay in the limo while Steve ran into the house for his dress shoes and a belt.

His parents' BMW was gone, but both Carrie's and Melissa's cars were in the driveway. He slipped in the front door, hoping to come and go unnoticed.

Carrie saw him and knew the look of a backseat tussle. "Hey, lover boy. What cha been doing? Or should I say who?"

"Not now, Carrie. I've just come back to pick up a couple of things."

"Who's the girl?"

"There is no girl. Micki and I went shopping, and I just needed to pick up my shoes and a belt for tonight."

"You brought that slut by our home. How dare you!" Her roaring anger came from nowhere. Carrie was sorry those thoughts had escaped her mouth.

"Once again, your mouth kicks in before you know any details. You are so wrong about Micki, but I'm not having this conversation with you right now. I have got to go! Bye!"

Melissa had heard them argue before, but she couldn't keep out of it this time. "You've got that stripper out in the car? Come on, Carrie."

Before Steve knew it, Melissa and Carrie were outside with Melissa screaming at Micki from outside the limo. Tim couldn't hear what she was saying, but he knew it was a lynch mob. Tim locked the doors, and Micki slid away from the door.

Melissa heard the door locks and went off again. "Listen, you slut. No locked doors are going to protect you from the truth. You were a slut three days ago! You are still a slut today, and you will still be a slut tomorrow. You will be a slut for the rest of your life!"

Tim had enough. It was time to leave. Micki was in tears. Tim drove as smoothly as he could to Verna's place. When they arrived, he couldn't get out of the limo quick enough to open the door for Micki. She sprang from the limo like a jack-in-the-box. Still crying, she ran inside and threw herself on the bed and cried.

Tim brought all her packages inside and then closed the door quietly. Sometimes his job wasn't easy. He forced himself not to return to the Donnatellis' home and turn a certain child over his knee and *Well, never mind*, Tim told himself. He just hoped he never had to drive Melissa anywhere for his new employer.

Steve arrived at the limo just as Tim was pulling away. He was devastated. He shoved Melissa, knocking her onto the grass. "What the hell do you think you're doing?"

From the ground, Melissa looked back up at Steve. "I'm trying to tell you people that she's trying to get into your pants so that she can get into your wallet. Men are so naive sometimes. She danced for Andy, but she couldn't seduce him so she went after you."

Carrie interrupted her. "Yes, he was, but she didn't go to him after her dance. And he said he didn't go to her."

"Carrie, you are just too trusting. She probably did Andy also. She's been coming onto guys for years. They don't even know that it's a trap. You, my friend, are the fish that got away." With that, she was up and heading back into the house.

Carrie and Steve looked at each other, knowing that they had messed up. Carrie voiced it after a few moments of silence. "What do we do now?"

Steve replied, "I think we've done enough for now, Carrie Donn."

George Williams sat in his office watching his workers prepare the Blue Ribbon Club for her customers. In the last couple of days, he had watched a murder and an attempted murder, and his life had been threatened. He decided that it was time to leave the business. He thought to himself, *You can't take any money with you.* What good would it do him to die wealthy?

George almost ran down the stairs from his office to the front business office. "Rosie, you're in charge until I return."

With that, he was out the door and on his way to the Frank Marcus Building at the Newark Airport Industrial Park. George was afraid of Frank Marcus but not enough to keep him from accepting his offer of four and a half million for the club and its property. That would take care of a few retirement bills.

When George arrived at the Marcus Building, he found that Mr. Marcus was taking the afternoon off . However, Richard Birch, his attorney, knew about the offer and closed the deal. George didn't even have to go back to the club. Mr. Birch wrote out the check and had George sign some papers, both knowing that it would take a while to close.

Richard Birch phoned Frank's son, Antonio, and asked him to take Sam Golden by to check out the club. Mr. Golden would check everything, from the stock to the girls.

Antonio had wanted the club for a long time, and now it was his. He could fill in his father when he joined him at the rosary. He couldn't believe that he was going to church in a few hours. How long had it been? He missed his boys' baptisms. It might have been their wedding.

Antonio was still smiling when he picked up Mr. Golden from the sixth floor of the Marcus Building. However, Sam was not smiling. He was supposed to be going home to take his wife over to his in-laws for an anniversary dinner. The more Sam thought about it, the better he felt about missing the dinner with his in-laws. Just then, a smile tried to crack his stern look, but he successfully fought it off . No one must know what he thought.

Meanwhile, back in Jersey City, Channel 4 was interrupting its regular programming. "Good afternoon. I'm Mike Shantz with Channel 4 News. We interrupt your ball game to bring you a special news bulletin from the White House. Ladies and gentlemen, the president."

"Early Saturday morning, I lost a friend and coworker. Congressman Joseph Roggerro died when his heart stopped. I have been told that his death may not have been from natural causes. If someone has murdered this great patriot, then there will be no rock big enough for him to hide under. I will not allow the snake to get away with this heinous crime. I have directed the attorney general to offer a one-million-dollar reward for information leading to the arrest and conviction of the person or people responsible for this abhorrent act. Let me also say this. When you attack a congressman, you attack America. I am declaring war on the individual or individuals that did this!"

"Well, ladies and gentlemen, that's it. The president really seemed angry. We've been told that the FBI will be handling all of the tips. The unknown individual and his or her helpers have now jumped to the top of the most wanted list. Once again, if you know anything, don't contact your local police. You need to call the FBI directly. This has been a Channel 4 News Bulletin, Mike Shantz reporting."

In a small motel room in Rolla, Missouri, Gail reached down to turn off the TV set. Channel 8 had carried the same bulletin. As she straightened up, she saw herself in the mirror and slowly touched her face as if it wasn't hers. When had the wrinkles come? The gray, she had touched up, but she hadn't noticed the wrinkles. Where had the thirty years gone? Almost on a dare, she and Sharon had left Missouri to seek the excitement of life in the Big Apple. They had both married well and divorced well. Then, for a while, love didn't seem as important as the rush. After a time, someone had introduced them to Dale Jackson, and he swooned her. He told her he was single, but she would find out later that was not the case. Still, she hung around him for five years until he died in the accident. Toll told her that he probably had done it on purpose. She hated Toll for that comment and for the way he had treated Sharon. He should have married her, but Sharon, too, hung around. Now they were both back in Missouri and not hanging around. Pug had dropped them off this morning. Their families didn't know that they were back in town.

If she were to turn Toll in, it would be like winning the lottery. But she knew that Sharon still had feelings for him. Sometimes, bad love seems better than no love, but it never is. As she thought about what he had done to Sharon, she decided to turn him in. Not for all of the things he had done to her and to others, but because of how he had treated her best friend.

Mr. Tolbert, the FBI will soon know who had the congressman murdered.

Johnny Trudle listened as Christi played a copy of the emergency police tape, and he smiled. He heard Toll threaten Mrs. Jackson and his admission to murdering her husband. Now Christi could get and was in the process of getting an arrest warrant for Billy Ray Tolbert. Johnny shook his head as he thought about his former job and partner.

Christina Douglas, a sultry tall blond who knew her business, had been his best partner. Now that was over. After a review of his actions with George Williams, he would be fired. Christi had hypnotic brown eyes and a body to die for. She kept herself in great shape because she didn't want anyone putting her down because she was a sissy. She worked at being tough and was. Marriage to her was something in her distant past. Johnny hadn't picked her as a partner. Christi had picked him. She knew he was married and had eyes only for his Pat. To her, Johnny was safe. She wanted to be a policewoman and not a token, always getting in the way.

Johnny was done for now because he needed to get on over to 5 Dunbar Place and be with his family for a while. The family was scheduled to be at St. Peter's by 5:30 p.m. "Hey, Christi, I'll get together with you after the service tonight. Okay?"

"No. I'll see you after the funeral. Take some time to be with your family and tell them I said hi and tell the governor we'll have to do tea again soon."

"Christi, you don't know the governor and you've never eaten with him."

"Yeah, but he doesn't know that. He'll go crazy trying to remember who I am."

"You have such an evil and twisted mind. No wonder I like working with you."

Five Dunbar Place was abuzz. Mary and Fran were finishing up their last-minute details and answering phones. The Roggerro family was not available for the time being. Beth had begun a supper meal for up to a hundred guests. Nick and Jere were both lost in working last-minute details. Tim had four limos ready with a police escort. Andrew was pacing. He hadn't heard from Micki, nor had anyone else.

Verna found Micki sobbing. A natural energy and intuition known as motherhood took over. She knew that Micki had crashed and burned. The old Western saying was that she had been thrown. It was time to get back upon that bronc and have another go at it.

Verna greeted Micki with her usual happy greeting, "Hi, Micki. How ya doin'?"

Micki didn't respond verbally to the obviously ridiculous question. She just took off both sandals and threw them at Verna.

Verna was smiling as she let the next shot fly. "Are we a little touchy about something tonight?"

"Go to hell! Shut up and leave me alone!"

"You didn't come back here for me to leave you alone. You came back here so that we could figure out what to do next."

Now for the first time, Micki made eye contact with Verna. Verna had her thinking, and Micki didn't want to think. She only wanted to cry and hurt.

"Bitch." She hated it when Verna was right.

"I'm your best friend and you call me a bitch. What do you call your enemies?"

"Stop it, Verna. It won't work. I'm unhappy, and I deserve to be."

"Girl, are you gonna let them win?"

"Who?"

"The ones who called you a slut."

"How'd you know that?"

"You live in a dreamworld some of the times. Did you think that everyone would be willing to overlook the fact that yesterday you were a stripper? Being a stripper's a pretty sleazy job. You've made a living off the oldest profession known to mankind. The congressman saw something in you and was willing to put his money on you. Now, because someone insults you, you're ready to give up. I can't make you go back and honor him with your presence at his service, but I can help you celebrate your return to your old lifestyle. Let me get us a couple of drinks, and we can get drunk and forget about Joe Roggerro. Maybe he was wrong?"

"You're still a bitch, but I love you. Help me get dressed."

"Deal." Verna smiled. She hadn't lost her touch.

Andrew was disturbed by the phone call from Verna, but he couldn't deal with it now. Steve, Carrie, and Tim were mute on the subject, so he didn't know if he would ever find out what had happened.

However, now it was time to leave. Mary, Fran, and Beth would stay behind while everyone else attended the rosary. James and Tim would be riding in the lead limo with Julie and Miguel Vargas. Nick's sons and some other young people would ride in the second limo with Nick and Ellen and the Durbins in the third limo. Andrew, Carrie, Steve, and Suzy would be in the last limo. As the convoy departed, it looked as impressive as any New Jersey had seen in a while.

Toll watched from his vantage point and saw that he would not be able to get a shot at the son of the man who had caused all of his troubles. For the next few hours, Andrew Roggerro was safe. He would not always have twelve policemen around him, and then he would join his father. A frown turned once again into an evil smile.

Hudson County deputies escorted the four black limos down the Belleville Turnpike heading east over to St. Peter's College. Andrew had never seen anything like it. They did not stop at any lights. Officers on motorcycles were blocking all of the ramps and intersections as they approached. The limos only slowed when they turned into St. Peter's.

Steve and Carrie had only said a couple of words to him since they had arrived. They hadn't spoken at all during the trip, but now was not the time to go there. Later, he would have to find out what they were so worried about.

Andrew was not ready for the next sight. Hundreds of reporters were taking pictures of the limos as they pulled into St. Peter's College. The chapel was at the rear of the campus, so the limos continued on. Surrounding the chapel area were perhaps two hundred police officers in uniforms. There were more plainclothes. Some were mounted. There must have been fifteen thousand people being held back by the police.

Well, they were staying behind barriers with the officers on the other side. National Guardsmen were interspersed among the police officers.

Andrew's eyes went to the chapel steps and saw a very beautiful, angelic form standing on the steps waiting for them. Micki was wearing one of her new outfits. The gray conservative suit made Micki look like a different person.

Carrie placed her hand on Andrew's knee and said, "Andy, give me a minute with Micki."

Before he could respond, Carrie had slipped out the door and was standing in front of Micki. All he could see was the back of Carrie's head. He wanted to know what was going on but knew not to disturb them. Andrew helped Suzy out and moved toward the rest of his family.

Carrie's eyes started to fill as she looked at Micki, knowing that she had misjudged her and how badly she must have hurt her. "Can we talk for a second?" Carrie was biting her lip to keep from crying.

Micki was startled at seeing Carrie pop out of the limo. Her fears returned quickly, and her courage melted. When Carrie spoke, it was with kindness and not the earlier venom. "This isn't the time or place."

Carrie ignored her response. "I . . . we have been wrong about you, and I am so sorry. I can't take back any of the hurtful things that were said earlier, but I am sorry. Please forgive me." Carrie extended a hand as a peace offering.

Micki took a chance and just reached out to hug Carrie. "Forgiven."

Out of the corner of his eye, Andrew saw the two ladies hug. Whatever had happened had a peaceful ending. Andrew walked forward, holding on to Suzy. Nick and Ellen fell in behind them, and they all entered the chapel at St. Peter's College. Bishop Dan Moore was there only to greet the family, and then he left. Father Jason and Father Mario would be able to handle everything. By the time they all had entered the chapel, they only had a few minutes together before the invited guests were allowed in.

Micki walked into the chapel with Steve and Carrie. Micki loved the incense and the music. Micki had never been in a Catholic church before. This one was small but very beautiful. The angels in the windows almost seemed ready to sing. It all seemed so grand yet simple. Words came out of her mouth that she hadn't planned on saying. "God, thanks for friends like Verna, Andrew, and Joe. Please take care of them."

Channel 4's ratings hadn't been as high as they currently were in a long time. Management believed that their coverage of the congressman's death was the reason. Thus, they wanted more. The evening news had a new lead story. It was a rosary being conducted at St. Peter's College.

Mike Shantz was ready with his white teeth and award-winning smile. The producer, Kim Watson, just shook her head and counted it down, "Three, two, and one. We are live, people. And, Mike, you are on." With her finger, she pointed to him.

"Good evening. I'm Mike Shantz with Channel 4 news. Sean Risen is live at the rosary service being held for Congressman Joseph Roggerro. Let's go to Sean now."

"Thanks, Mike, and good evening, everyone. I'm standing as close as security will allow. Unless you have a pass given out by the family, you cannot cross this line. What's amazing, Mike, is that no one is trying to. Sure, there are security forces all around us, but everyone has been respecting the line.

"The family arrived about an hour ago and had a little time alone inside with Father O'Raley. The other guests were allowed in at 6:00 with the service starting at 6:30 p.m. There's a convoy approaching now, and that will be Governor Cardetti. Even the governor has been low-keyed about all that's been happening. He's arriving now so as to be as small a distraction as possible."

"Sean, just how hard was it to get an invitation for tonight?"

"Mike, someone said that you almost had to have come over on the boat with Giovanni from Sicily to get one. It was really tough. There isn't much space inside the chapel, and this is their choice of place to conduct the service. They actually attend church at St. Joseph's, but the congressman was really involved with this school."

"Thanks, Sean."

"As we speak, Father Jason O'Raley is conducting a rosary service for New Jersey's senior congressman, the late Joseph Roggerro. There will be a funeral service tomorrow morning where the president is expected to say a few words. We will be following all that is going on while respecting the wishes of the Roggerro family that we cover it from a distance." Then the newscast went on and covered the rest of the city's and world's events.

Kim Watson knew that tonight had been a hit and that tomorrow would bring in more viewers.

When the rosary was over, the Roggerro "family" was escorted to their limos. The governor's limo had lined up behind the other limos. Within a few minutes, they all sped off toward 5 Dunbar Place. All who had come were invited to the congressman's home for dinner. With lights on, the convoy stretched out with twenty-six cars heading toward 5 Dunbar Place.

Andrew's limo was silent. The reality that Joe Roggerro was gone from them had sunk in now. Suzy was holding his arm and trying not to cry any more. With the police escort, they were home quickly.

As Andrew and his party were getting out of their limo, a strong and commanding voice stopped him. "After supper, son, we've got to talk. But for right now, introduce me to your friends."

The governor was so taken with Micki that he didn't even hear the others names. Carrie broke the governor's spell by announcing a powder-room break. Three new friends, Carrie, Micki, and Suzy, scampered off to safety.

As the ladies left, one member of the governor's security force walked up. "Governor, we have movement on the perimeter. Could I get you to move your conversation indoors?"

Surrounded by security personnel, Andrew moved inside to the banquet hall. Nick had been waiting for Andrew to make his entrance before he announced, "Ladies and gentlemen, dinner is served. Please bow with me as Father Jason offers grace."

James Silver escorted Andrew to his seat, fortunately a few seats away from the governor. As Andrew took his seat, Jason began his prayer. "Heavenly Father, we are here tonight because Joe was taken from us this week. We thank you for his life and for his love of life. Bless this food to the nourishment of our bodies. In the name of the Father, Son, and Holy Spirit. Amen." There was a large shuffling sound as the sign of the cross was made by a hundred plus people.

All of this seemed so strange to Andrew. Two hundred people were eating supper in his house, in his banquet hall that he didn't have a couple of days ago. He was mourning the death of his father when his father was sitting just a few seats over. The hall was beautifully constructed with marble from Sicily. There were paintings in the room worth more than he dare think about. The china actually came from China and the crystal from England. The governor was here today, and the president would be coming tomorrow. But why was he here, now? Andrew wondered why he was the focus of attention instead of Joseph Roggerro.

Andrew knew the people around him, but he wondered who all of the others were, and he wondered who he was. Had Joe helped all or most of them? Did he help them financially as much as he helped Micki? What would they expect of him now?

As he ate, Andrew's eyes scanned the room, stopping on Frank Marcus. He had met Mr. Marcus and his son Antonio sometime back, but that meeting was all fuzzy now. They were dressed very nice, but Mr. Marcus seemed sad. There were stories about him that Andrew hadn't paid much attention to until tonight. People almost seemed afraid of him. He made a mental note to ask his father about him later.

Finally, the girls returned from their never-ending powder-room break. All eyes were on them now as they took their seats. Andrew thought it felt like they were on a fashion runway. It seemed like some were ready to break out in applause. They were the prettiest in the house.

One thing that bothered him was that everyone seemed to accept the fact that he was the congressman's son. Had they all known? He wondered how much they really knew about him and how much they were making up in their own minds. His stomach growled at him, and he wondered how much he would be able to eat.

Andrew had finished about half his plate when the governor whispered to him, "Can we escape to Joe's office for a moment? I need to run something by you?"

"Certainly, sir." As they made their way out of the room, Andrew saw that Johnny had a big smile on his face. Andrew knew that there was no way that the governor would offer him his father's congressional seat.

Toll had left Jack and Milo behind to watch the Roggerro home. For Milo, this was as close as he had ever come to combat. He was too young for Vietnam, but lying there in the tall marsh grass and bushes, he felt as if he were in combat. He held a modern semiautomatic rifle with a scope that allowed him to shoot at objects more than five hundred yards away. Since they had returned from Mexico, Jack had been quiet and moody. Milo was almost afraid to ask him anything, so he just lay there, watching the Roggerro house, 5 Dunbar Place.

The governor worked at looking casual. He lit a cigar and sat on the corner of Joe's big desk. After a few polite conversational questions, he began with his true agenda. "Andrew, have you given any thought to who might be a good replacement for your father's seat in Congress?"

Andrew couldn't believe his ears. How did Johnny know what was going to happen? "Governor, I have no idea. I haven't been connected to what my father was doing. He hid the fact that he was my father so well that I didn't know he was my father until after his death. I wish that I could change that, but you can't go back and undo things now."

"Son, I know that this is not a good time to talk about this, but you need to consider filling his seat. We don't need to lose another seat to the Republicans. You don't have any experience, but you have name recognition, and that will get you elected. Later, you can get the experience. Your father didn't have any experience when he started. He just started."

"Sir, thank you, but no thanks. I'm going to be taking over my father's businesses. You'll need to find someone else."

"I'm sorry, son. I know that I can be pushy, so let's just continue this conversation some other time."

"I'll agree to that." Andrew was relieved to be free from the governor's glare.

When they walked back into the hall, the governor was all smiles. He seemed to give a nod to a few in the crowd. Was he just waving, or was there a signal somewhere in those waves? Andrew began to feel that he was becoming paranoid.

Milo had his safety off with a round locked and loaded in the chamber. His finger was on the trigger and ready for some action. Toll hadn't wanted any action, just observation. Jack noticed some movement at the front door and peered into his scope. Milo took it as a signal to fire at will. In a matter of three seconds, he had fire twenty rounds at the front door. For Milo, it was the greatest feeling that he had ever had.

The sharpshooter on the roof fired twice, but the first bullet had ended Milo's life. A shot through the temple had scrambled his brain, and he was dead. The other agents and deputies were charging toward the sound of the shots. The Secret Service agent on the roof had seen one other person in the brush, but he could not find him now.

Jack never heard the sound of the two bullets that took out his friend Milo, but he saw the results. There was no doubt that his friend was dead. Jack took about three deep breaths and then forced himself to move. He had frozen in fear, and it was only the fear of him taking a bullet that made him roll and roll. He hopped into his white Mustang and headed for the loop.

The movement that Jack had seen was the governor's security checking the area before the governor's departure. Because of the large distance, there was a delay in the sound of Milo's firing. People just started dropping. Then the automatic fire sound was heard. Manny Shapiro spun and fell. He grabbed his head. Marge and Bev Marcellus fell to the ground as though someone had just let out their air. Ron Nelson turned as a bullet whizzed by him and found a column. The impact made an exploding sound, shooting plaster everywhere. Then there was silence except for radio jabbering. Dr. Becker would be busy again at Christ Hospital.

The governor soon departed once it was determined that one shooter was dead and that the other one had fled. Nick and Jere took care of seeing the rest of the guests off. Carrie had decided to sleep over. Suzy was willing to share her room.

Andrew and Carrie slipped off to be by themselves for the first time. For Andrew, it had been the longest day of his life. For a few moments, they just sat on the sofa in the game room. Then Carrie made Andrew take off his jacket and lie down with his head in her lap. She leaned down to kiss him softly and then moved away. Andrew responded to her kiss and wanted more, but she put a hand on his chest and pushed him back.

"I love you, Andy, but that's all that you get tonight. I just wanted to distract you from some of today's events."

"That wasn't very much of a distraction. I need to be more distracted." It was working. They were both laughing now.

"Shall I call and see if Micki is willing to dance for you again?"

"Are you never going to forget about that?"

"Probably not. How about you?"

"Probably not." They both laughed some more.

She played with his hair, rolling it with her fingers. He rambled on about all of the things that had happened in the last forty-eight hours. Soon, both were fast asleep.

Mary Bright had been worried about Andrew and had started looking for him. She smiled as she saw the two sleeping on the sofa. It amazed her how many good things could be happening in the middle of chaos. As she covered them, she thought about how long and hard tomorrow would be.

CHAPTER

Tuesday, June 5, 2001, would not be just another day in Jersey City. More people were expected to be in town than at any other time in the history of the city. The governor and the president could draw a crowd as well as bring a crowd. Three hundred National Guardsmen had been called in. The Secret Service had been on guard duty all night long, keeping certain areas secure. The press corps numbered several hundred. No hotels could be had within a hundred-mile radius. Life in Jersey City would not be business as usual.

At around five in the morning, Andrew rolled onto his side and found Carrie lying next to him. He had never felt anything quite as good as the feeling he had at that moment. His plans had been to get up at six, *So why change them now*, he thought. With an arm draped over her midsection, Andrew drifted back asleep.

His movement had awakened Carrie, but she liked how she felt also. She had finally found someone that only wanted to be with her. A tear came to her eye as she thought about the coming events for the day. A good man had died and was going to be buried today. That man was Andy's father. She too closed her eyes. She wasn't ready for the day to start or to lose the warm, comfortable feeling she had.

Police Sergeant Christi Douglas shook her long blond hair and watched it ripple in the mirror. She seldom wore makeup, but she would today. A congressman was dead, and she was working his case. There was no telling whom she might run into today. She had arranged for the warrants as Johnny had suggested, but he wouldn't be serving them with her. He might not ever work again as a cop. He lost his cool. Cops can't lose that. Lives depend on them not losing their cool. It had become way too personal for Johnny. She chided herself for not getting him off the case. She knew it would become personal with Johnny. She told herself, *Today is today and yesterday was yesterday. You just have to go forward.* Then she went back to the hair for a few final strokes.

Toll was alone now. He had murdered Jack when he found out about Milo. The others had taken off, not wanting to end up like their coworkers. Toll's money had been good, but it looked like it was drying up. Pug and the girls had disappeared. Now it was just Toll.

No one would find Jack, and no one would miss him, Toll thought. Having no one to talk to didn't seem to bother him as he enjoyed his own company. Who else was worth his time? He thought that maybe it was better now that he was alone. Nobody would be messing up his chances of getting Roggerro.

Father and son had caused all of his problems. His life was running so smooth until those idiots had to play around with his money. Now the police were looking for him, but soon others would be looking for him as well. Toll knew that the Roggerros had caused all of his woes. Joe was dead, and his son was not far behind. At this thought, again Toll smiled. *Soon, young Roggerro, you will pay for messing with Toll.* He laughed out loud until he almost cried.

Billy Ray Tolbert had given in to his insanity. His world was a dream now that revolved around him. Sex, power, and drugs had lost their appeal. One evil thought drove him, and it might come to fruition soon.

In a quiet and remote part of Jersey City, Father Jason pulled down a long drive to a nice but dark-looking home. The sun was not yet up, and the street lights weren't helping. He just felt in his gut that he shouldn't be there, but he was. Frank Marcus had called and asked for the meeting, but it all seemed wrong. Jason wasn't even sure how he got the call. It should have been another priest. Jason knew he was the wrong person for this visit. He had heard too many confessions involving Mr. Marcus to have any doubts about his profession. He was still wondering why he was there as he knocked on the door.

A priest is not completely holy. Their feet sometimes want to head away from where they were called to go. For Jason, this was one of those times. He only got one knock in before he spun and started home. Mr. Marcus would have to solve his problem without a priest today. Jason's mind was really on the funeral that he was in charge of in about four hours.

Before he had gone two steps, a voice spoke to Jason from the dark shadows of the door. "Good morning, father, won't you come in?"

Jason paused. The voice didn't sound like a bad person. Still, Jason did not want to face the man that may have been responsible for Joe's death.

Frank Marcus stepped out from the shadows and held out a welcoming hand. "Please, father, come in."

Jason still didn't move. His thoughts were still in favor of leaving. For some, he thought, there is no hope. Marcus's gray hair looked distinguished. His dark brown eyes seemed gentle. No, it was a mistake to come, and he started to leave once again. Flashes of Jonah kept coming to his mind. Our enemy is not necessarily God's, he thought.

Jason just knew that he needed to get away from this man and this place. "Mr. Marcus, I've made a mistake in coming here this morning. In a few hours, I'm going to do the funeral of my best friend. Word is you had him murdered in order to stop his crime bill. You may deserve a priest, but not this one. God's sent the wrong priest."

Tears started down his cheek before he could turn to get away from Frank Marcus. As he turned, Mr. Marcus stopped him in his tracks with, "I had nothing to do with Joe's murder. And, because you are

Joe's best friend, you are the perfect person to come. God doesn't make mistakes, but we do."

Back at 5 Dunbar Place, Fran brought in breakfast for both Carrie and Andrew. They were both still sleeping on the sofa. She looked down on them and smiled. Both Fran and Mary Bright had followed Andrew's life. Joe and Jere talked about him all of the time. Joe could be completely free with his feelings in Jere's company, which oftentimes meant in Fran's or Mary's presence. Today would not be an easy day for Andrew, but it needed to get started. After setting down her tray of food, Fran woke him up just like his mother had done these twentysome years, by tickling his feet with her fingers.

At the other Roggerro household, Ellen was laying in bed, not wanting to get up. Her thoughts were on her three sons. She had tried to spoil them some. A mother wonders how much is too much. Nick asked her to give up her job at Tony's of Fifth Avenue, and she did. She still managed to get a design or two over to Tony's from time to time. But most of her time had been spent raising three sons. On this morning, she was worried only about one of them.

Today was going to be hard enough for Andrew without the whole world watching him as well. Ellen wished that only the family could attend, but she understood why that was an impossibility. She had lost her best friend, Marie, twenty-seven years ago, and now Joe was gone as well. Again her thoughts returned to Andrew. She wondered if she had done as well, raising Andrew as Marie would have.

Out in the guest house at 5 Dunbar Place, Micki had Tina's music blaring. "Private Dancer" had made her number one in Micki's book of life. The beat and the passion had a way of helping her cope with anything. Today was not a day that she was looking forward to, but Joe deserved to be honored, and she would be there.

As she lay there, she thought about his death. Was she the reason he was dead? *If he hadn't come by to check on me or if I had quit earlier . . .*

oh it's no good trying to undo something that has happened, she thought. Micki wondered if the killers would have found a way to do their dirty deed if it hadn't happened that night.

Listening to Tina had always helped her when she was down, so Tina got louder. Micki slipped off her top and laid it next to a phone message that she hadn't noticed yet. The message was from Melissa, asking her to ask Steve about Marcie. With Tina belting, Micki stepped into the shower.

Jere hadn't slept much, nor was he ready to get out of bed. If he got out of bed, then Joe was really gone and not coming back. He almost believed that if he didn't get up and go to Joe's funeral, then Joe might still come back.

It's for moments like these that God provides a partner. Demri gave him a sharp elbow to the ribs and told him to get into the shower and not use all of the hot water. Painfully, Jere rolled over and out of bed. He had tried to keep from starting, but the day just wouldn't listen.

By 7 a.m., 5 Dunbar Place was alive with movement, but the silence was deafening. People were showering and dressing. Most were getting ready for the funeral, but few were talking. Things were getting done that needed to happen, but it was very quiet. Tim was driving Carrie home to allow her to get cleaned up. As Andrew walked around, he thought he was living in an anthill. People were scurrying along with their individual tasks all for the greater good and all without making a sound.

Pug had dropped off Gail and Sharon in a small town in the Missouri Ozarks. He promised to return soon, but he needed to check on a few things first, whatever that meant. They both needed some coffee to clear the cobwebs. Gail poured the coffee and started the conversation, "Sharon, I didn't sleep well last night. My mind has been on certain events in New Jersey."

"Gail, honey, you've got to forget about that. We no longer are a part of it."

"I'm talking about your friend Toll."

"If he were my friend, I wouldn't be here. Let's leave him in the past. If he knew we were here, he might try to come and get us."

"I can't. I keep thinking that he had something to do with the congressman's death. He was really angry about the bill that he was working on, and I think he either killed him or had someone else do it. You know that Jack and Milo took off for Mexico real quickly after the congressman's death. Just maybe there's a reason for their quick departure."

"That kind of thinking will get us both killed. Don't ever mention those things again."

"Sharon, I'm going to use a payphone and call that hotline number to the FBI. I'll just tell them to check up on him."

Sharon didn't like it, but once Gail makes up her mind, she will carry through with it. Sharon scowled but didn't say any more.

Channel 4 News had its highest viewer share ever during the last couple of days. The reason was their coverage of the congressman's death.

Today, they would expand their coverage a little bit more. More viewers translates into more money. For the station, more money is good.

"Good morning, I'm Mike Shantz with a special edition of Channel 4 News. We are not going to New York this morning. We are going to keep it right here in New Jersey because the world is coming to Jersey City today."

"Let's go live out to St. Peter's College and speak with Channel 4's own Sean Risen. Good morning, Sean."

"Good morning, Mike. Let me review for our viewers the events that have transpired over the last few days. Just after midnight on Saturday morning, June 2, Congressman Joseph J. Roggerro was pronounced dead by ER doc Morris Becker. The cause of death is still being investigated as we speak. Just last night, Father Jason O'Raley conducted a rosary for the congressman's family and close friends. Only two hundred people were allowed into the chapel. Our governor was among those attending, and he will be back for the funeral. And now today, Tuesday, June 5, 2001, Congressman Joseph J. Roggerro will be laid to rest in Holy Name Cemetery right next to the college.

"Mike, last night during the rosary, there were more than a hundred thousand people out here. They all stayed behind the barriers where we've been told to stay. Most just stood looking at the chapel where the rosary was being conducted. Some sang, and some just laid flowers. They were all told to go home after the service, but thousands have returned. Today, I'm told that speakers will carry the service out here, but no reporters are being allowed inside the chapel. The Secret Service and National Guard are here providing security along with Jersey City's finest."

"Several world leaders expressed interest in either coming or sending someone to represent them, but they were told, 'Thank you, but no thanks.'

The president is coming, but he is only bringing a small group from the Hill."

"We picked up a rumor that there will be a dinner with some of the foreign diplomats later today, but that location has not been given out to the public. Let me send it back to you, Mike. I'm Sean Risen with Channel 4 News, reporting live from the St. Peter's campus."

"Thanks, Sean, and great job. Let me tell you that Congressman Roggerro has served his country well for almost thirty years. We have a duty to report to our public all that we can. At the same time, Joe Roggerro has a family that is grieving over their loss. We will cover as much of the funeral and surrounding events as we can without violating their space.

"We have just been told that the congressman has a son that has lived with his uncle since the death of his mother and sister. This will be a coming out for the congressman's son. We've been told his name is Andrew Roggerro."

It was working. The ratings were going through the roof. Other national networks were plugging in. The CEO was hearing *caching, caching.*

Back at 5 Dunbar Place, folks were wrapping up their last-minute details before going to the funeral. Beth was supervising breakfast and thinking about two different parties after the funeral. Two hundred guests would be returning for a reception. Two hours was a short time for an Italian dinner, but it would have to do. Next, Beth would be in charge of preparing an international meal for the foreign diplomats that had come to pay their respects. The meal would be based around chicken with all of the dietary restrictions that faced her. Still, she was going to the funeral.

The Roggerro family had already started showing up even though their departure time was over an hour away. Either Fran or Mary was working the door with James. Everyone entering had to be cleared.

Andrew was thinking that his museum was just about at capacity, and that amazed him. This was his house now. He didn't know if it would ever be his home. He couldn't think about that right now. Right now, he needed to hug his mom and dad.

Micki came into the big house to have some coffee. Her little guest house had a kitchen, but she didn't want to be alone right now. She picked up a phone message from Melissa, but she couldn't think about anything else right now. Right now, she needed some coffee. In the dining room, she found a sort of motel-like buffet. She was not the only one interested in some coffee and maybe a little food. Nick's boys and Jere's family were helping themselves. Micki just blended in with them.

Steve hadn't come out yet. She wondered what she really felt for him. Her thoughts also went back to Saturday night. Someone bumping into her reminded her that she was in Joe's home but without Joe.

Nick walked over to check on her. "Micki, are you doing okay?"

Micki wasn't sure whether to tell the truth or not. "I think I am. No, I'm not. So much has happened in such a short time. Nick, what am I doing here?"

"You're here because Andrew wanted your help. You're also here because Joe cared about you and you, him. When he saw you, he wondered about his daughter—what she would have been like and what she might have looked like. Micki, you are here because Joe would have wanted you here."

"Nick, I see two nice families, and I can't stop thinking about what I used to do for a living. You can't really want me here?"

"Micki, people are going to remind you of your past, but I won't. Joe cared about your future, and that's what we care about. I'm never going to forget that you saved Andrew's life."

Micki walked over and kissed Nick's cheek. "I could get used to this family stuff ."

"Thank you for joining Channel 4 News with our full coverage of Congressman Joseph J. Roggerro's funeral. And now, with some insider information, we join Nicole Hammer live just a short distance from the Roggerro home. Nicole, what do you have for us?"

"Mike, we are as close as you can get to the Roggerro home unless you are a resident of the area or you have a special pass. I just spoke to someone on the inside, and they said that most of the family would be gathering here before proceeding to St. Peter's College Chapel. The congressman loved this school and asked that, when he passed, that they use this chapel for his funeral. On a different note, I asked the name of the dancer that the congressman had gone to see, and they told me her name was Micki. I understand that for the present time, she is staying in the guest house on the Roggerro compound."

"Nicole, do you know why she would be staying there?"

"My insider didn't feel like they should tell me any more for the time being. I can tell you that a number of cars have come to the Roggerro home this morning, including Governor Cardetti."

"Thank you, Nicole. We'll get back to you later.

"In about ten minutes, a caravan of limos will depart 5 Dunbar Place en route to St. Peter's College where the funeral will take place.

The funeral is scheduled to begin at 10 a.m. The Secret Service has told Channel 4 News that the president will in fact be attending the funeral. He is scheduled to arrive ten minutes before the service starts and will leave right after the service. Congressman Joseph J. Roggerro will be laid to rest next to his father and mother."

Not even Father Jason was allowed to be alone with Joe. The Secret Service, with their bulging jackets, were not about to leave the congressman for any reason. The president of the United States would be in this chapel in less than two hours, and their job was to keep it secure. Only the governor and Roggerro family would not be checked with a metal detector because they would have been checked before they started their convoy. All other guests would have to submit to the metal detectors.

Thus far, Channel 4 News had covered several areas in their program. A few dignitaries were taped arriving at the Newark Airport. They had discussed the immigration of Giovanni and Estella Roggerro from Sicily in the late '30s. Congressman Roggerro had gone to St. Peter's College for his BS in Business. His interests in the American legal system had led him to Rutger's University and an LLD in law. Channel 4 News had revisited the car accident that had happened twenty-seven years earlier, taking the lives of the congressman's wife and daughter.

Perhaps their luckiest moment was when Governor Richard Cardetti agreed to be interviewed live. Just before he left his hotel, Governor Cardetti met with Mike Shantz for an interview that would be played right before the funeral.

"Good morning, everyone, I'm Mike Shantz visiting with Governor Richard Cardetti. Good morning, governor. How are you doing?"

"Good morning, Mike. We know each other well, so let me get right to the point, and then I need to go. Today is not about politics. Yes, New Jersey lost a congressman, but more importantly, she lost a good friend. Joe Roggerro was my good friend. Whenever I needed a tough question answered, he would give me his honest opinion. We didn't always agree, but I never questioned his heart. New Jersey, and the nation for that matter, needs to pray for the Roggerro family right now. There is nothing tougher than losing someone you love. I'm not sure how much your viewers know, but young Andrew just lost his father, but twenty-seven years ago, he lost his older sister and his mother."

"Thank you, sir. We have covered that some, but I'm sure that we'll revisit that story. Sir, what can you tell us about all of these dignitaries that are arriving from around the world?"

"The Roggerros said that they wanted this to be just a family thing, but the world is not listening. Several countries have sent delegations to express their sadness over the loss of this quiet world leader. I've spoken with the Roggerro family, and we will have a reception for them, but the location isn't being released."

"Governor, thank you for your time, and our prayers do go out to the Roggerro family."

"Let's go out to St. Peter's College and Channel 4 News's Sean Risen."

"Hello again, Mike. I'm beginning to feel like a sardine. As we pan the area, there's just a sea of people. The guardsmen are doing their best to keep the road open for those who will be attending, but it's becoming increasingly difficult. St. Peter's College has set up several speakers so that we can hear what's being said, but the Roggerro family refused to allow any cameras inside the chapel."

"Sean, what's the mood of those attending?"

"Mike, the mood is somber. Congressman Roggerro is not a sports hero or movie star, but he's amazingly popular. There are people here from all parts of America. Mike, when you serve in Congress for nearly thirty years, you are doing something right. Roggerro may have made a few enemies, but he only has friends here today. I'm Sean Risen with Channel 4 News, live at St. Peter's College."

Toll's stomach turned over as he thought about all of the flowery bullshit coming out of that biased, liberal newsman's mouth. What did he know anyway? Insanity can turn anything into something useful.

Billy Ray Tolbert was following the news accounts, hoping to find a time when he could snuff out the life of his enemy, Andrew Roggerro. And, if he were lucky, just maybe, he could kill that dancer as well. Once again an evil smile appeared on his face as he spoke to no one. "Mr. Roggerro, I can wait for you. Soon, you'll go to join that Boy Scout of a father of yours."

Both Mario and Jason were ready to greet the family. Jason had planned the order that they would enter the chapel and have a moment alone with Joe. Private moments included the Secret Service watching your every move. Normally, the grieving family is the last to arrive, but they had requested a closed casket service, and this afforded them one last good-bye.

Tim pulled the long limo up to where a Secret Service agent motioned for him to stop. They opened the door for Andrew before Tim could get out and do it. Andrew didn't wait for Steve and the ladies; rather, he led the parade into the chapel. Once inside it, Andrew couldn't move. Jason read this and came to him. Taking Andrew gently forward, Jason led him to the front of the chapel, and then Jason walked away.

Andrew was looking at his father for the last time. It was as if he had stepped into another zone. Everything faded away except his father in front of him. Andrew surprised himself by reaching down and touching his father's hands. This was the body of his father. He knew it wasn't his father, but this was all that he had left. His breath came with great effort. Andrew placed an elbow on the casket to help support himself. His whole body began trembling. As if cued by an angel, Carrie walked to him and held on to Andy, her Andy. He cried as he thought about all that he had lost. He cried thinking about all that his father had given up to serve his country. Now this great man was gone. Still unsteady, he leaned over and kissed Joe's forehead.

"Dad, I'm sorry that I didn't trust you more. I'm sorry that I didn't go with you every time you invited me. I'm sorry that I didn't know you better. What I'm finding out makes me very proud. Take this picture of our family, and know that I will try to make you proud of me." Andrew and Carrie slowly walked over to the mourners' section, just out of view of those who would be attending. Not able to see because of his tears, he allowed Carrie to lead him. In that moment, Andy was saying good-bye to what had been and was entering his future.

Nick and Jere came next. Jere needed help from Nick to move down to the front. It was as though his body were not connected to his legs. They refused all his directives. Nick gave a tug and Jere started forward and together they faced Joe.

Nick spoke first and in Italian, "You know that Momma and Pappa are glad to see you, but we miss you here. I still need you. Andy still needs you. I hope that we did okay by you raising him. Say a prayer for us, won't you, brother, my brother, my brother, my big brother?"

Jere didn't understand a word of what Nick had said, but he acted like he had. He could only pat his friend's hand, and then they moved on.

Demri and Ellen locked arms and then went forward, seemly drawing strength from each other. They stayed only a moment, and then they joined their men.

Next, Suzy walked slowly down the aisle. In a few months, Jason was to have married them, and she would have walked down this aisle for a different reason. Life changes quickly. She placed her hands on his and looked at him, knowing this was her last look. "Joe, if you can hear me, I need to say a few things. Don't feel badly about leaving before we were formally married. You see, each time that you held me, I felt a part of you. A formal wedding would have been nice, but it wouldn't have made me love you any more or feel closer to you. I will miss you every day that I may live, but I'll never be sorry over losing you. You have made me the happiest that I have ever been. The only thing that we were missing were children. I'm going to borrow Andrew from time to time, and he said that I can have some grandmother time with your grandkids. Honey, just know that I love you, now and forever." She kissed him and turned to find Jason beside her. He led her to a seat next to Andrew.

Jason motioned to Mario to send Micki. She walked quickly down to the casket and began her speech. "I'm not sure what to do or say exactly, but you know that you were the most important person in my life. You made me face myself and my lifestyle. I work for Andrew right now, and one day, I'll work for me. If I could've picked a father, I'd have chosen you. Joe, I'm afraid now, but I'm going forward. If you can help me in any way from there or know someone to put me in contact with, I sure would appreciate it. You know I never kissed you before, but I'm going to now so get ready." With that, she leaned over and kissed Joe good-bye.

Now her tears came in great gushes. Her legs felt as if they were about to give way when Father Jason took her by her arm and said, "Let me walk you to your seat." Holding her arm, they slowly moved away.

She looked up and whispered, "Thanks, Joe."

Jason heard her, but he didn't hear her clearly. "Did you say something?"

"You're welcome.

The rest of the family and the staff passed by and were seated. Next, two funeral home workers came down to the front and sealed the casket. And, on Father Jason's cue, the old pipe organ began playing hymns. Two ushers opened the large double doors at the front of the chapel. Most of those entering were of Italian descent, including the governor and his family. Mr. Frank Marcus and his family seemed to stand out. The Military Honors Team was present but off to the side and virtually invisible.

At 10 o'clock, the doors came open and in whisked the president of the United States, John Ashcroft, and his wife. The speaker of the house and two other legislators followed the president. All of the aides stayed outside. Andrew had not met this president, but he knew that he would before the day was over.

The organ continued playing very softly as all eyes turned to the podium. Father Jason stepped up to the mic and began the service that no one was looking forward to. "On behave of the Roggerro family, let me welcome you. I think you know, but let me remind you that only the Roggerros will be going to the grave site. Following this service, everyone in this room will be welcome to join the family for a reception at one this afternoon at Joe's home.

"Shall we join our hearts and minds in prayer? Holy Father, we gather here today to say a formal farewell to a friend, brother, and father. We ask your blessings on all that we do here. All that we do, we dedicate to you for what you have already done for us. Amen."

The parish responded with, "Lord, hear our prayer."

Jere stood up and walked up to the mic like he knew what he was doing, full of confidence. "Friends, family, and Andrew, I wanted to tell you a little bit about my relationship with Joe. We were like brothers, but even closer than brothers. Joe may have told some things to Father Jason, but almost no one knew all of the things that Joe was involved in. Yes, he was your congressman, but he was your neighbor as well. He's very well-off, but he gave away more trying to help people help themselves.

"Joe was not without his faults, but on the night he left us, he was trying to help one more person. He had just gotten enough votes to send his crime bill to the floor for a vote. But it was still important to him that he stop by for another visit with a friend to see if he could talk her into changing careers. That's why he was there, and he was successful. There are more stories in this room where Joe stepped in and helped out in a tough situation. Perhaps if I asked who among you has Joe helped, none would be sitting.

"Twenty-eight years ago, Joe was elected to Congress. He served his country well, but he never left the Jersey City area. He never stopped caring about you and your families. One person can have an impact on his surroundings, even a nation. Like you, because I knew Joe, I have been blessed."

Most often in a Catholic worship service, the congregation is very quiet with only an occasional whimper from a baby. However, today's service was very different. Many were crying, and some were responding verbally to Jere's remarks as if they were alone with him instead of being in a chapel filled with mourners.

As Jere moved away from the mic, Andrae Crouch and Natalie Cole stepped up to their mics to sing Joe's favorite hymn, "My Tribute."

Natalie spoke, first looking at Mary and then to Andrew. "We give honor to the pastors here, to our president and his wife, and to you, Andrew Roggerro. We dedicate this song to Joe, a good and faithful servant."

> How can I say thanks for the things you have done for me.
> Things so under served, yet you give to prove your love for me.
> Th e voices of a million angels could not express my gratitude.
> All that I am and ever hoped to be, I owe it all to thee.
> To God be the glory;
> To God be the glory;
> To God be the glory for the things he has done.
> With his blood, he has saved me.
> With his pow'r he has raised me.
> To God be the glory for the things he has done.
> Just let me live my life.
> Let it be pleasing, Lord, to thee.
> And should I gain any praise,
> Let it go to Calvary.

Andrae and Natalie went on several more minutes, repeating different parts of the song. When they sat down, you could have heard a pin drop. What had been tears had turned to smiles on most. After just a moment, the president moved to the podium. "I know, Andrae, that you wrote that song before you knew Joe Roggerro, but it certainly fits the Joe Roggerro that we all know. Thank you, and thank you, Natalie.

"I'm standing before you today because Joe was my friend. I also know that he was your friend. But I'm standing here as the leader of the greatest and most powerful nation in the world because I was Joe's friend. He told me that I needed to be the next president, and that he would do everything in his power to see that it happened. Well, here I am, Joe, and it's because of you.

"Joe has gone to heaven, but he has left a son. Andrew, will you be the next congressman from New Jersey? Joe's gone, but not really. How many smiles did he give out? How many did he share his faith with? Did he ever give you a hug or tell you a story? Joe is not gone. He has touched us all, and we will never be the same. I think Joe would want us to go and touch others. Thank you."

A cellist from St. Peter's College began very softly playing "Near My God to Thee." She was joined by the rest of St. Peter's String Ensemble. Thirty minutes had passed already, and it had only seemed like a moment to Andrew. He realized that he had forgotten about Suzy and Carrie. Suzy was crying again, so he held her close. Carrie also hung on to his other arm.

Father Mario read portions of the Gospel according to John, the fourteenth chapter. Next, he read most of the eighth chapter of Romans. Then Father Jason stepped back up to the mic. "Good morning again. Of course, you know why we're here. It's just difficult to stand here today, knowing that my best friend is no longer walking around down here with me. When I was told that Joe had died, my heart almost stopped beating. *I wonder, How many people will actually miss Joe Roggerro?* The malls are open, and tourists are all over New Jersey. Does it matter what we do here on earth?

"Twenty-seven years ago, I attended the funeral of Joe's wife and daughter. For part of the service, I held three-month-old Andrew. I thought that, if God could let this happen, then I wanted nothing to do with him. Actually, Joe was the person that brought me back to church. Joe changed lives wherever he went. Minutes before his death, another person decided to change their path in life. There are too many cases for me to recount, and Joe wouldn't want me to. I know of one person's life who changed after Joe's passing.

"You have been addressed by the president of the United States. He is the leader of the most powerful nation in the world. With a word from him, flags across America were lowered in Joe's honor. Congress recessed for the day. Leaders from around the world have come to Jersey City to pay their last respects to their friend. Friends, Joe was a friend worth having, and yes, one person can make a difference here on this earth. America is a better place because Joe was here.

"Permit me to change gears here for a moment." Jason looked right at Andrew, and all eyes followed. "Andrew, I know that you have many questions about why? Don't worry, so do I.

"As a pastor and friend, let me tell you what I do know. Joe had a personal relationship with God through Jesus. For the most part, he lived by God's precepts. St. Paul knew that we would be afraid of meeting death, so he wrote to tell us not to worry that Jesus had already overcome death. In short, death is only scary if you don't have Jesus waiting for you on the other side. Jesus knew that it would be tough on all of us. That's why he told us not to worry, that he had gone to prepare a place for us, and he would have it ready when we get there. Friends, that sounds pretty good to me!

"Let me say that I believe that someone took Joe early. His business was not finished here. Yes, God could have stopped it from happening, but he didn't. We must live with what is and not with what could have been. Someone, maybe someone here today, needs to carry on the work that Joe has started. The crime bill must be passed. These people cannot win!

"What are you seeking in life? Seek first the kingdom of God, and everything else will fall into place. Joe believed this. He lived it and knew that everything else would take care of itself. Believing can cost you a great deal. Joe's life is an example of why and how to do it. My friend was not perfect, just willing."

Jason raised his hand and bowed his head and prayed. "Heavenly Father, today we thank you for sending Joseph Roggerro into our lives. I pray for healing and comfort for those who knew and loved him. In the name of the Father, and Jesus Christ his Son, and the Holy Spirit. Amen."

The congregation responded again with, "Lord, hear our prayer."

Jason sat down. He had made it through the service, and he was still holding back his emotions. He could breathe for a moment. The honor guard moved to their positions around the casket. Removing the flag, they began to fold it in a slow and professional manner, as was their custom. The stillness was amazing. After they finished, one airman held the flag up for Col. Jackson to inspect. Then Col. Jackson accepted the flag. The airman saluted in slow motion and then returned to his position. Col. Jackson approached the president. He held the flag as though it would break. Then as the airman had, Col. Jackson saluted the flag, very slowly, and then moved away.

Andrew was not prepared for what happened next. John Ashcroft walked over to Andrew and went down on one knee. He handed him the flag as he said, "On behalf of a grateful nation, I would like to present you this flag. Andrew, the nation will miss your father's work, and I will miss him. I am truly sorry for your loss."

The Secret Service escorted the presidential party out. The honor guard then moved to their pallbearer positions.

Fathers Jason and Mario exchanged places with Mario addressing those in attendance. "We would ask that you exit through the rear of the chapel at this time. The Roggerros will meet everyone at 1:00 p.m. Thank you for being here today."

For the first time in his life, Andrew felt really lost. On his right arm he held Carrie. On the other was Suzy. No words came to him. His mind was dull and not functioning. He stood but didn't move. There were some pats on his shoulder and words were said, but he didn't hear them. Andrew just stood there. His eyes filled, and his breathing grew heavy, but he didn't move.

Tears rolled down his cheeks, but he didn't move.

Out of the corner of his eye, he saw Suzy looking at him with a little smile. He could smile, but he had nothing to say. They were rolling his father away, and he couldn't move. He lowered his head with his hand coming up to his face as if to cover the tears. They weren't just rolling away his father but also his mother and sister, and he cried.

As the bagpipes began playing, Suzy and Carrie started forward, and Andrew moved with them. Exiting the side doors of the chapel, they followed the honor guard. Outside, it was raining, so there wasn't the bright noontime sunlight. Andrew wasn't prepared for the lights of the cameras and the flashes. Still, he focused on his father's casket and kept walking. While the mood of the thousands outside was somber, they began to applaud. Andrew kept walking.

They passed through the cemetery gate and stopped at his father's plot. There were two headstones there. Joe would be placed next to Marie's. The rest of his family gathered, and he felt Nick's hand on his shoulder, and he was glad.

Only Jason used an umbrella so he could protect his Bible. He began, "The Bible tells the story of a holy man coming to a small village. The whole town came out to see who was going to receive God's wrath on that day. Samuel had told Jessie to be there and to bring his sons. The holy man looked around and said that there was one missing. Jessie assured him that it was just little David the youngest and he was watching the sheep. Samuel said that they would wait while they fetched him. Most of the people figured that he had gotten into trouble again, but now he would die. Samuel didn't come around for small stuff . Finally, the little boy showed up and walked right up to that holy man and said, 'Wassup?' Okay, that's not exactly what he said." Some laughed.

"The holy man said that he had been waiting on him to join them. Then he asked David to take a knee. Samuel opened a flask and poured oil on David's head. Then he looked at the young man and said that God had chosen him to be the next king over the children of Israel. With that, the crowd was astonished. David thought that it sounded good, but he had no idea of what was to come. David was not afraid of God or the holy man. He chose to serve his father and try to do what God had for him. God has a plan for each of our lives if we will listen to him. Joe listened. He tried to use his talents to honor God and serve his country. God uses us to change situations for the better. How many people did Joe ever turn away? None that I'm aware of. God's blessings most often come thru us.

"David had many ups and downs. David never doubted God, but I'm sure that he disagreed with him from time to time. David did go off on his own from time to time and found some really sticky situations. Sometimes bad things did happen to David when he was following God's leadership in his life. But God never left him alone. Joe was sent to heaven early, but God never left his side. Just know that God used Joe in a mighty way. Joe walked with God here, and God received him there in heaven. We too need to walk with God now so that we can do his will and know that special peace that passes all understanding and comes only from him."

"Hear now David's words as translated in the NIV:

The Lord is my Shepherd,

I shall not be in want,

He makes me lie down in green pastures.

He leads me beside the quiet waters,

He guides me in the paths of righteousness for his name's sake.

Even though I walk through the valley of the shadow of death,

I will fear no evil, for you are with me.

Your rod and your staff, they comfort me.

You prepare a table before me in the presence of my enemies.

You anoint my head with oil; my cup overflows.

Surely, goodness and love will follow me, All the days of my life,

And I will dwell in the house of the Lord forever. Amen.

"From dust we come and to dust we return . . ."

Andrew had heard most of what Jason had said and then suddenly realized that it was raining. He looked left and right, and both ladies were still holding on. Then Jason closed in prayer.

Andrew watched as the honor guard raised their rifles to the sky with seven firing three times each. As harsh as that sound was, the horn blowing taps was soothing. His father's day was done.

From behind him, Nick handed him a rose. Instinctively, he placed it on his other father's casket and said bye. Suzy and Carrie held on as they carefully made their way back to the limos. None of the people had left; the crowd was still there. Tim opened the door, and they got in.

A nervous Carrie asked, "Are you okay?"

Andrew had a dazed look like he was somewhere else. He managed a nod.

Sitting across from him was Suzy. She smiled through her tears. She thought that he would be okay, but he had just buried his father.

Andrew looked out his window and saw Johnny. A flash of anger shot through his body. He wanted the bad people to pay for this. He kept his thoughts inside and just waved at Johnny.

Johnny was thinking, *I'll get them, son. I promise.*

One last time, the cameras panned the limos as they were pulling away. Toll watched the news clip and spouted some words that only he understood. His insanity was still growing. "That Roggerro has been lucky so far, but his luck is about to run out." Then he laughed his insane laugh. Now it almost sounded like a wolf howling at the moon.

Micki didn't take the limo back. She just wanted to walk. Johnny walked a little ways with her, but then Christi found him, and they parted company. Micki was wondering what had just taken place. *A great man has just been laid to rest and now what am I supposed to do?* She walked all the way down to Liberty Park, took the ferry, and rode out by the Statue of Liberty. As she looked at her, she thought a lot of people came here for a second chance. *Maybe this is my second chance?*

Johnny hadn't let anyone know how angry he was, but Christi knew. "Christi, Father Jason knows that these guys have got to be caught. We can't allow them to win!" Johnny thought but didn't say, *They aren't going to win. No matter what it costs me.*

Johnny was now willing to cross the line. Before someone can cross the line, they must be willing. After crossing the line, everything becomes cloudy and gray. He was approaching territory that officers of the law face daily. Today, Johnny was willing to break the law in order to uphold it.

Gail picked up the phone to dial the FBI hotline. Her hands were shaking, and she knew that this call could kill not only her but also Sharon. She ran to the bathroom and lost her breakfast. She returned to the kitchen and once again picked up the phone and dialed.

"Hello, you've reached the FBI's hotline. I'm Leslie."

"Yes, Leslie, will my information be confidential that we talk about right now?"

"Agent Amy Woods spoke into Leslie's earpiece. "She's using a phone at a rented house in Rolla, Missouri."

Leslie simply nodded to Amy. "Yes, this call is as confidential as you want it to be. What information are we talking about?"

"I think I might know who killed the congressman. Who pays the reward?"

"The FBI will pay the reward if your information leads to the arrest and conviction of those guilty. And if you are the only one giving us the main information, you will get all the reward."

"I'm not doing this for no damn reward, but if he finds out that I've told, then he'll have me killed. So I might as well get the money if I'm takin' all these risks. Right?"

Leslie already had all of the information she was about to ask for, but she didn't want Gail to know it. "Let me set you up a meeting with an agent. I'll need you to give me your full name, number, and address."

"Do I have to?"

"Only if you want the reward."

An hour later, Agent Thomas Cox of Rolla interviewed Gail and was satisfied that she knew what she was talking about. The FBI now wanted to speak with Billy Ray Tolbert. A fax was sent to Agent Amy Woods, and she started the process that would make Toll the number one person on the FBI's most wanted list. By 1:30 p.m., the Newark agency had received the new top ten list with Billy Ray Tolbert of Jersey City at its top. Now a second arrest warrant was issued, but this one was a federal warrant. Billy Ray Tolbert had become the number one suspect in the murder of Congressman Joseph J. Roggerro. While Toll's insanity was growing, his space to move around in was shrinking.

In spite of the security, guests at 5 Dunbar Place were happy to be there. With the Secret Service gone, it was easier, but not easy, to enter. The Jersey guard was out in numbers, helping the county deputies provide security. After getting past them, James Silver and Mary Bright would welcome them and help them forget about getting inside the house.

Micki returned from her trip, again having second thoughts. She looked around, and everyone seemed to know each other, except she didn't know any of them.

Fran broke into her thoughts, "There you are, dear. You have a phone call." With that she handed Micki a portable phone and walked off.

"Hello?"

"Micki, this is Melissa. Before you hang up on me, I need to tell you one word. Marcie."

With some edge on her voice, "Is that supposed to mean something to me?"

"Only if you have feelings for Steve."

"Okay, I give up. Who is Marcie?"

"You'll have to ask Steve." With that, the phone went dead.

Fran Weekly approached Micki with a young lady. "I believe you were just asking about Marcie. Marcie, meet Micki. Micki, she's looking for Steve. I think he's in the game room. Would you show her where it is?"

Micki was surprised by the turn of events, but now her curiosity took over and she replied, "I'd be glad to."

Andrew and Carrie had slipped into his bedroom to rest for a few moments. Nick found the two sleeping children with contented smiles on their faces. He hated to wake them, but he thought the show must go on. With just enough of a touch on Andrew's shoulder to wake him, Nick said, "Our guests are waiting, son. Let's let Carrie rest. Just come on down."

"Sounds good, Dad.

Andrew looked at Carrie and hoped she truly would be his wife one day, but there was no hurry. Right now, he needed to get downstairs.

Johnny and Christi were going over all of the information that they had when his cell phone rang. No name came up on caller ID. "This is Johnny."

"Detective Trudle, this is George Williams. I'm ready to talk. I've sold the Blue Ribbon, but meet me there in fifteen minutes. I'll be sitting in a dark blue Ford Expedition."

"I'll be there. Let's go, Christi."

Even though they were not supposed to be together, she took off. She would deal with the captain later. "Where is he?"

"The Blue Ribbon."

When she phoned in her destination and asked for backup, Toll knew that Williams was going to talk. Two and two will equal zero. Toll turned off his police scanner and sped off to the Blue Ribbon Club.

When Andrew entered the large dining room, he saw a seat next to his father that was probably saved for him. He also noticed Frank Marcus and his wife sitting off by themselves. On a whim, he joined them.

"Good afternoon, Mr. Marcus. May I join you?"

"Certainly, Andrew. Allow me to introduce my wife, Lori."

Nick was surprised by Andrew's actions, but he thought it was the same thing that Joe would have done. Without another thought, he welcomed everyone and invited Father Jason to offer grace.

Micki actually found Steve standing next to the pool and staring at the guesthouse where Micki was staying. Marcie ran up to her fiancé and gave him a long, welcoming kiss. It had been just long enough for Micki to walk up behind them and push both into the pool. With a whirl, Micki was gone.

Marcie spoke first, "What's gotten into that bitch?" Steve's silence spoke volumes. "Did you sleep with her?"

Again, Steve said nothing. In fact, he hadn't slept with her, but he had wanted to.

Marcie took his silence as a yes answer. "I take it you hadn't told her that you were engaged?"

Finally, Steve spoke, "Everything that you've said is true." He then lowered his head and became silent again.

Marcie made her way out of the pool, grabbing a towel, and sloshed out of 5 Dunbar Place. Along the way, a ring dropped from her finger.

Christi spotted the blue Expedition first and then floored it.

She surprised Johnny with her action. "Hey, what cha doing?"

"He's not moving, Johnny! He should've looked at us by now. Something's wrong."

"Damn it! They must've heard you call for backup."

Christi didn't lose the second police car. They may not have caught on, but they were staying with Christi. As she pulled up, Johnny jumped out of the car like he was going after a doggie at the rodeo. There was a bullet hole on the driver's side window, and all the doors were still locked. Johnny broke a rear window and unlocked the doors. Together, he and Christi pulled out a dead George Williams

Johnny hadn't noticed his arm bleeding. He was just focusing on George. A shot to the head had ended his life about five minutes earlier. Frantically, Johnny administered CPR, but there was no response at all.

"Johnny, we're not going to revive him. You need to stop!" With a nod to the backup team, Christi helped pull Johnny off Mr. Williams.

Howie Daniels called for an ambulance and reported the murder to the central station. Christi walked Johnny into the Blue Ribbon so he could calm down and clean up his wound.

Chief Dave Jennings reported to the scene and went straight to Christi's car to check the video of the whole incident. As he was finishing, he saw Christi returning from the club. "Christi, where's Johnny?"

"He's still inside. He got cut getting into Mr. Williams's car."

"Tell him to get his ass out here right now!"

Christi spun around and reentered the club. "Hey, partner, the chief is out there, and he wants you."

"Tell him I'll be out as soon as I finish my drink."

"Come on, Johnny."

"Just tell him."

Again she returned to the chief and delivered Johnny's message.

The chief was outraged. "Get him, Douglas, or get his badge, it doesn't matter."

A few moments later, she returned with Johnny's badge and gun.

The chief took them and passed them to Howie. "Get these back to the office." With that, Chief Jennings got back into his car and drove off.

Verna had only been asleep a couple of hours when her phone rang. "Yeah. Hello."

Micki hadn't been thinking about Verna and her hours of work. She'd only been thinking about how confused she was. "Verna, this is Micki. Did I wake you up?"

Verna was still very sleepy, but she liked joking around so she replied, "Yeah. Hello."

A twinge of guilt hit Micki, so she decided to get off the phone. "Listen, Verna, I'm gonna hang up and let you sleep."

"Yeah, like I'm really going to go to sleep now. I'm going to lay here wondering why you called."

"Okay, Verna. He's got a fiancée."

"Micki, do I know who we're talking about?"

"No. Does it matter?"

"Nope. How'd you find out?"

"She walked right up to him and laid a big, wet one on him."

"That's when you walked out of his life?"

"No. First, I pushed 'em both into the pool. Then I walked out of his life."

"And?"

"Why do I feel so bad?"

"Let's do dinner, dear. Right now I need to sleep. I go in at 8:00 p.m., so pick me up at 6:00."

"Thanks, Verna. I love you. Bye."

James Silver came over to Andrew and announced, "Sir, Mr. Donnatelli wishes to have a word with you. I told him this was not a good time, but he sounded rather agitated."

"Excuse me please." He had enjoyed visiting with the Marcuses and didn't want to leave. He made his way out of the hall to see what was so urgent with Steve.

Andrew looked at Steve with a look that said the house had better be on fire.

Steve looked back with only embarrassment on his face. "Andy, I know you're busy—okay, overwhelmed! But I needed to tell you that I can't stay here. I have to move back home. We can talk more later."

Again, Andrew looked back, still agitated. "Okay, Steve, but this is kind of abrupt. When did you decide this?"

This was not a question that Steve was going to enjoy answering. He stood there as he had stood in front of his mother about to tell her the embarrassing truth. He held his hands in his pockets and lowered his head and let the embarrassment begin. "While standing in the pool with Marcie."

Andrew motioned with his hands that there was a whole lot more. "Okay, and . . ."

"We were in the pool because Micki brought Marcie out to me and Marcie greeted me with a kiss . . . you know, tongue and stuff . Then Micki pushed us into the pool."

"Okay, and . . ."

"Okay. Uh, me and Micki, uh, kind of, uh, had a thing starting up."

"Until your fiancée showed up?"

"Yeah, kind of like that except I don't have a fiancée anymore." With that, Steve lowered his head and left.

Andrew didn't have long to wonder about Steve as Jere called to him and told him the guests were starting to leave. Andrew stepped into the reception line next to Nick and thanked his guests for coming. As people passed, they each seemed to squeeze his hand a little firmer than they ever had before. It was like they were seeing a little bit of Joe in Andrew.

Frank Marcus had waited to be last. "Andrew, the business that I used to be in no longer exists for me. Your father succeeded with me as well. Lori and I will be taking our first real vacation back to Sicily in a few days. Until I see you again, you take care."

"Bye, Mr. Marcus and."

Frank gave Andrew a big bear hug, catching Andrew completely by surprise. Andrew didn't get to finish his sentence.

Frank left, wiping his eyes. He loved Joe like a brother, but they never were able to enjoy each other's company. Those days were behind him. He knew that his other extended family could end his life at any moment. But with each day he had left, he planned to donate his time in helping his city and family.

It had stopped raining, but it looked like it could start up again at any moment. Her long blond hair blowing in the wind, Christi looked like a model posing for a shoot. Actually, she was mustering up enough courage to go back into the Blue Ribbon. Finally after several minutes, she walked into the bar to tell her partner good-bye.

Johnny stood at the bar, kind of spinning his glass. Then he looked down into it as though it held the answers. But there were none there. Their witness had just been carted off to the morgue.

"Forget him, Johnny. Other clues will turn up." She was only saying that to make herself feel better. Johnny was not impressed with it. He had been her mentor for the last couple of years. He had become her friend, but now she had to tell him something that would separate them, maybe for good. "Johnny, you're too close to this one. You've got to let us handle it."

"I know you had to say that. But you also know when I'm going to stop working on this case. Just keep me up on what's happening."

"Aft er what happened here today, that's impossible. You're going to have to stay away from me for a while or I'll be out of work as well." Christi walked out of the Blue Ribbon dazed by what had just happened. She loved working with Johnny, but now he was off the force. As the door closed behind her, a portion of her life ended.

Johnny didn't speak. He couldn't. He just tipped his glass. Johnny was taken back twenty-seven years ago when his sister and niece were murdered and no one was ever charged with the murder. Now Johnny gave up trying to find Joe's murderers as a cop. From now on, he'd be looking on his own.

Ruth poured another, Johnny's third. "You're the cop who's looking for the congressman's murderer. This one's on the house."

Christi got into her police car, leaving her partner behind. She had done her duty. But now she was sick to her stomach. Maybe she was too close to this case as well. It felt like she was getting another divorce. She needed to back up and evaluate whether this was still a good profession for her. Interrupting her thoughts, the fax started spitting out a new fax. Central was sending her a fax, listing Billy Ray Tolbert as the prime suspect in the murder of the congressman. She would put her vocation changes on hold for a while. Maybe she could find this Tolbert.

In no time at all, Nick had the staff setting up the hall for the international visitors. While Nick was directing traffic, he noticed the governor capturing his son.

"Hello, Andrew, my boy."

"Hello, sir."

"Andrew, can we talk somewhere?"

"Sir, what do you know about the crime bill?"

"I have a general idea. Your father showed me his major points. I don't know the fine details though."

Andrew turned to Jere and asked, "Uncle Jere, can you join us in the office for a few minutes?"

Jere had no idea what was going on, but he was willing to listen. "Sure."

Responding to the doorbell, James opened the door to find a beautiful young lady dressed for a night on the town.

"Hi, sir. I'm Rachel Schloop. Is Mr. Roggerro in? I need to speak with him."

James Silver was irritated by the question but charmed by the person. Her innocent-looking smile made it difficult for him to refuse her request. Ma'am, unless this is very urgent, I'll need to have you come back some other time.

We're all very busy right now."

"Well, okay. But I'm Andrew's doctor from Christ's Hospital. His father, Nick, said that he wanted to know the results of the tests that we were running on Joe Roggerro as soon as they were back. We gave a copy of the report to the police, and I kept a copy for Nick and Andrew."

"I'm sorry, doctor. Please, do come in."

As James entered the office, Governor Cardetti told Andrew, "It sounds great to me, and we can announce our plans to the public tomorrow at a news conference."

"Certainly, sir. Will you introduce me or do I just get up and speak?"

"I'll introduce you, son. But don't worry about the details. My staff will take care of that."

James felt he could interrupt the meeting at this point, "Excuse me, sir. Dr. Schloop is here to see you."

"Please, James, show her in here."

"Yes, Andrew."

Andrew was very surprised to see a beautiful young lady walk into his office. "Hi, Rachel. You look wonderful. I've not seen this side of you."

"Andrew, I tried, but they wouldn't let me wear this in the ER."

"Rachel, let me introduce you to Governor Cardetti and a family friend, Jere Durbin."

Rachel nodded to both, but she was focused on her business, so she didn't waste any time. "I'm sorry to disturb your meeting, but I have the congressman's test results. He was given a drug that caused his heart to stop."

Andrew was not surprised and took the news well. "Thanks, Rachel. I would have been surprised if that weren't the case. It only confirms what we all had grown to believe. Thanks for bringing it out here. And you look good in black, but I thought doctors always wore white or green?"

"I have a life outside the hospital. I was going on a date when they paged me about the results. I canceled the date and delivered the results."

"You shouldn't waste all that effort. How about staying for dinner with us? We have some guests coming, and my brothers would love to have your company."

"You don't have to, but I'm really hungry."

"James, how about sitting her right between Pete and Mike?"

"Certainly, sir."

All at once, limos started arriving again at 5 Dunbar Place. The world had gotten smaller during Joe's life. He had friends all around the world, and now they were coming to say farewell. The governor and

Nick greeted guests at the door. They came from Europe, both eastern and western. The visitors came from several parts of Africa, Arabia, Asia, and the place down under. Some were not friendly at home, but in Joe's house, all was put aside for the moment.

Nick had the tables set in a large circle so that everyone would be facing each other. During the evening, each delegation had a chance to speak, and many left gifts for Andrew. Andrew was treated as if he were the crown prince. To the guests, he was. They had developed a relationship with Joe that had gone way beyond ink and paper. Joe had demonstrated that he truly cared for them and their futures. Andrew learned a little more about his father.

Christi had also taken Johnny's gun when she left the bar. He hadn't really minded. It put an end to his law-enforcement career. As a civilian, you weren't supposed to have a gun in a bar, and he was a civilian now. He was sipping his fourth when his cell rang.

"Johnny, this is Christi. How ya doin'?"

"I thought you told me to stay away from you?"

"You are. This isn't my phone. It belongs to a friend. So how ya doin'?"

"Four drinks better."

"Are you going to stop soon?"

"Soon. You didn't call me to talk about my drinking habits. What do you have for me?"

"Someone has pointed a finger at Billy Ray Tolbert. The man in the field who starting shooting was working for Tolbert. All we have to do is find him. Also, the results are in from the drug tests run on the congressman. He was drugged at the Blue Ribbon. Williams was probably going to name who gave the drug, but they probably worked for Tolbert. The owner of the trucking company, Mrs. Jackson, is talking about her late husband's activities, including laundering money. I've gotta go for now. Get out of that place. That's an order."

"I love you too. Bye."

"Ruth, could you call me a cab?"

While the last of the guests were ushered to their limos, the staff was cleaning the hall one last time. The final function had ended. Fran and Mary were still answering their phones, and the house was being restored to just a home again. Many small miracles had taken place to make everything happen, and now it was time to go home.

Nick looked at his son and saw a man. Andrew had transformed during these last few days. Both men just looked at each other and sighed. Nicked hugged his son and said, "Good night. I'll see you tomorrow."

Johnny didn't tell Christi, but he had one last stop to make before returning home. The cab stopped in front of Frank Marcus's house, and Johnny got out. He paid the cab driver and sent him on his way.

Security knew Johnny was there before he rang the doorbell. "Yes, officer, how can we help you?"

"I'd like to speak with Mr. Marcus for a minute."

"If you don't have a warrant, then . . ." Lucio received a message in his earpiece that Mr. Marcus would see the guest. "Okay. Mr. Marcus will see you." Lucio didn't like all of the changes that were going on. In the past, no police officer would have ever thought of entering Mr. Marcus's home.

The home from the street seemed pretty normal, but once inside, Johnny was amazed at its size. The entryway had been dark, but then the house became bright.

Frank Marcus knew of Detective Trudle and hoped he was not a suspect. "Good evening, officer. What brings you by my home?"

"Mr. Marcus, I'm not here as an officer of the law. I retired today. I just came by to get some worries off my chest. I don't believe you've had anything to do with recent events. But your contacts might know more than we do. I'm worried about Andrew. I thought I could protect him, but now I don't know. I've lost a sister, a niece, and now Joe. I don't want to lose Andrew. If there's any information you can share with me, I'd be truly grateful."

"Let me have your card, and I'll call you if I find out anything. Tell me what you know."

"We think it's a Billy Ray Tolbert. We have several connections. We think that he attempted to kill Andrew at the Blue Ribbon. The other night, one of his drivers took several shots at Andrew at his residence. The FBI believes he's responsible for Joe's death. I'm just grasping at straws. Thanks for your time. Bye."

Frank Marcus appeared to be unmoved by Johnny's information, but it unnerved him. Lucio saw the change but said nothing. He just escorted the officer out.

Mary and Fran had already closed down the house office. Julie and Beth had closed down the house. Finally, there was some stillness in the big house at 5 Dunbar Place. Andrew walked into his room to find Carrie watching a movie. He suggested he take her home, and she agreed. "I'm so tired. I'll need to let Tim drive us."

"Andrew, you don't have to go with me." She didn't mean it, but she felt she had to say it.

"Come on, Carrie Donn." As they were leaving, they waved to a just-arriving Micki.

Andrew returned to his big home and went straight to his bed. He still wasn't sleeping in the master bedroom, yet. He had many things on his mind as his head hit his pillow, but none of them mattered because he was out as soon as he was prone.

As Toll awoke, he noticed that it was pitch black. He didn't know where he was. His insanity began to wane as pure terror raced through his body. His whole body was sweating, and he still couldn't see. He could hear breathing, so he asked, "What's going down, and who are you?"

A voice whispered, "Mr. Tolbert, I believe I told you to leave the young Mr. Roggerro alone. Why didn't you listen?"

Toll wanted to strike the person next to him, but he couldn't move. Something was holding him in place, and his hands were stuck on the steering wheel. "I've stayed away from him."

Marty took off Toll's blindfold and looked into a pair of eyes that knew fear. Toll wasn't used to being on the receiving end. "Mr. Tolbert, when I found you, you were in a hotel room that just happens to be right across the street from city hall. I believe you were checking out your rifle when we stunned you. I'm sure you didn't know that there was going to be a news conference there tomorrow."

"What'd you do to my hands?"

"Super glue. We expect it to dissolve in the Hudson."

Toll was ready to end this man's entertainment. "Just do it!"

"Good-bye, Mr. Tolbert. Enjoy hell." Marty gave the signal and got out of the rig. It began rolling down toward the Hudson. There were guard rails there, but they couldn't stop a big rig.

Toll was alone and going to meet death. Then a smile appeared as he remembered the road on the right, just before the river. He might just make the turn. At worst, his rig would turn on its side and not go into the river. They thought they were so smart, but they had forgotten about the road at the bottom.

The rig was going too fast, so he pumped the brakes. Nothing happened. He pumped again and nothing happened. He had no brakes. He would have to just roll it and see how far his rig would slide.

As Toll approached the bottom of the hill and the road, Pug pulled out a little and flashed his bright lights. In an instant, Toll swerved left on reflexive actions and plunged into the Hudson. In that second, he knew he was dead. If he had hit Pug's rig, he would not have gone into the river. But he missed Pug's rig. Then he hit the water. Marty had left the windows down, so there wouldn't be any air pockets, just cold, deep water.

Pug headed for the New Jersey turnpike and Missouri. He thought he might be able to find a job driving down to Texas from time to time. He might even hook up with Gail. He thought, *I'll cross that bridge when I come to it.*

From a payphone about an hour later, Marty dialed 911 and reported that a rig had just gone into the Hudson at River Road.

Andrew had gone down to the entertainment room. There, Beth brought him some coffee, a roll, and the paper. Still, he turned on the TV to catch the morning news.

"Good morning from Channel 4 News. Again today we are going to keep it right here in Jersey City. Yesterday, New Jersey buried one of her own. The longtime Democrat Joseph J. Roggerro was laid to rest in Jersey City. The president had offered a hero's tomb in Arlington, but the Roggerro family said that he belonged here. His father immigrated to this country from Sicily right before the outbreak of WWII. The coroner's office has issued a statement saying that the congressman had indeed been murdered."

"In another late-breaking story, let's go to Linda Stone down at the water front. Linda, what do you have for us?"

"Good morning, Mike. The lead suspect in the murder of Congressman Joseph Roggerro was the manager of Jackson Trucking. Last night, there was a 911 call reporting that a semi ran through the barrier and sank into the Hudson. A salvage crew has just pulled out one of Jackson's trucks. The chief of police will not give us any more information at this time, but if that rig contains Billy Ray Tolbert's body, then the FBI will have to find another number one for their top ten. If that is Billy Ray in the truck, why did he do it? Did he feel the pressure of a nationwide hunt or what? We may never know."

"Linda, let me get this straight. They have recovered the rig and a body?"

"No, Mike. There was no body, but the truck belonged to the trucking company that he managed. Many are wondering if he drove into the Hudson to avoid being arrested. The police have released a tape where Tolbert admits he killed his former boss. It was only a matter of time before he was found."

"From across the river, we have a question from Katie. Good morning, Katie. What's your question?"

"Good morning, Mike. You guys have been busy the last few days. Wasn't Billy Ray Tolbert the lead suspect in the murder of Congressman Roggerro?"

"Yes, he was, but we didn't know that until yesterday afternoon."

"If his body is found and identified as the person in the rig, then your city and state will be able to relax a bit."

"You're right. That would answer the big question. He had motive and the desire, but the exact how and by whom may never be answered."

"Good job, guys, and thanks."

"That was, of course, Katie from the other side of the Hudson."

"Alex, tell us what you know about the ten o'clock news conference."

"We know that the governor and the son of the late congressman will be holding a news conference at city hall. The mayor would not release any other details at this time. We can speculate that it has something to do with filling the congressman's seat in the house. The governor will be there as will Andrew. Our sources tell us that Andrew and the governor have spent a lot of time behind closed doors and that he has, in fact, asked Andrew to replace his father."

"Alex, do your sources have an answer?"

"If they knew the answer, they weren't giving it to me. They did say that we shouldn't miss the news conference."

"All right, thank you, Alex . . ."

Andrew decided he needed to meet with his staff and pass on what Jere had revealed to him about his father's wishes for his staff .

When they were all present, he began. "I thought you might want to know about our future together. I want you to feel free to take any new job offers that might come your way. Personally, I am not going to change anything for one year. During that time, I'll determine what I will keep and what will need to go. For example, this was my father's house, not mine. I don't know if I want to live here. If I do stay, the whole staff can stay with some tasks modification. For example, most of the time, I will drive myself, etc., etc.

"Now, about my personal life, it will stay that way, private. You may have figured out that I care a great deal for Carrie, but she will not be staying here.

"For the time being, Micki will be staying in the guest house. My father thought of her like a daughter. I would like her to be treated as if she were my sister. I don't know if she will stay working for me or go into business as she and my father previously discussed.

"Next, my father left notes for the staff in case he should die unexpectedly." This was not easy for Andrew to say. He paused for a moment and then continued, "First, Tim is to pick any of the cars in the garage, and it is to be his. Mine is there, and you can't have it. It's the little gray one. Secondly, Julie, Miguel is to have his undergrad tuition paid as long as he's passing. If he goes on, we can talk about that. Beth's two teens are to have the same deal. My father has stated that he would like you to stay with me. He has an account set up for each of you, and it is now worth about $100,000 each. You can have it now or leave it where it is.

"Finally, I want some peace and quiet, so I want everyone to go away for a week. I have instructed Fran to give you an additional five thousand for you to go and play. Thanks for helping me in a very tough time. I also know that you really did it for my father, but thanks.

"James, before you leave, I want a key to the house and the codes.

"Beth, I'm not eating lunch here today. The governor has invited me to dine with him, so you may take off now as well."

The staff melted away, and 5 Dunbar Place became very still.

www.ingramcontent.com/pod-product-compliance
Lightning Source LLC
Chambersburg PA
CBHW050453110726
47899CB00003B/921